Voting at Fosterganj

Ruskin Bond has been writing for over sixty years, and now has over 120 titles in print—novels, collections of short stories, poetry, essays, anthologies and books for children. His first novel, *The Room on the Roof*, received the prestigious John Llewellyn Rhys Prize in 1957. He has also received the Padma Shri (1999), the Padma Bhushan (2014) and two awards from Sahitya Akademi—one for his short stories and another for his writings for children. In 2012, the Delhi government gave him its Lifetime Achievement Award.

Born in 1934, Ruskin Bond grew up in Jamnagar, Shimla, New Delhi and Dehradun. Apart from three years in the UK, he has spent all his life in India, and now lives in Mussoorie with his adopted family.

RUSKIN BOND

Voting at Fosterganj

Published by
Rupa Publications India Pvt. Ltd 2017
161-B/4, Gulmohar House,
Yusuf Sarai Community Centre,
New Delhi 110049

Sales centres:
Bengaluru Chennai
Hyderabad Kolkata Mumbai

Copyright © Ruskin Bond 2017

This is a work of fiction. Names, characters, places and incidents are either the product of the author's imagination or are used fictitiously and any resemblance to any actual person, living or dead, events or locales is entirely coincidental.

All rights reserved.
No part of this publication may be reproduced, transmitted, or stored in a retrieval system, in any form or by any means, electronic, mechanical, photocopying, recording or otherwise, without the prior permission of the publisher.

P-ISBN: 978-81-291-4494-2
E-ISBN: 978-93-5333-554-0

Sixth impression 2025

10 9 8 7 6

Printed in India

This book is sold subject to the condition that it shall not, by way of trade or otherwise, be lent, resold, hired out, or otherwise circulated, without the publisher's prior consent, in any form of binding or cover other than that in which it is published.

Contents

Introduction — vii

The Old Lama — 1
The Long Day — 4
Home — 11
At the Bank — 17
Monkey Trouble — 25
Snake Trouble — 37
The Kitemaker — 51
Most Beautiful — 56
Voting at Fosterganj — 65
Landour Bazaar — 74
A Night Walk Home — 83
Foster of Fosterganj — 87
A Magic Oil — 91
The Garlands on His Brow — 97
A Guardian Angel — 103
The Zigzag Walk — 110
The India I Carried with Me — 113

Introduction

There is a sense, that many of those who live in cities share, that life in the smaller towns, away from the glitz and glamour of the modern urban life is strangely quiet and uneventful. Nothing could be further from the truth. By virtue of being a dweller of one of these so-called quiet places, I can say for sure that not a day goes by when there is not some excitement that upturns the gentle rhythm of life if even for a short period of time.

Telling the stories of the people who live in small places carries its own dangers. Most people know each other by name or reputation if not more intimately. Now, however, with the constant influx of tourists and those in search of a spot of calm, there are plenty more unknown faces that one sees on the roads and cafes. Many a time there has been a knock on the door and I opened it to find a small child holding out a book to be signed or some not so small men and women who want to come in and hold forth on their love of books.

Yet it is in describing the people who live here, their concerns and the drama in their lives that I get a lot of pleasure. The Fosterganj of the title has a motley collection of characters, many of who appear in my book *Tales of Fosterganj*. Election time here is a chance for everyone to air their grievances knowing they are going to be heard only once in five years. Now, there are cell phones that ring with calls and messages from canvassing politicians. Even till a few years back, though, it was all completely dependent on meeting the voters and convincing them that putting their stamp on a particular election symbol would be a good way to end much of their woes.

Another place where I find that a lot of locals tend to gather and have much to discuss, is the bank. The bank manager is someone everyone knows. Unfortunately, he too knows everyone a bit too well—their account balance that is. Yet, most managers I have met have not been the straightfaced businesslike city bankers. Here there is time for a cup of tea, for others to stroll in and discuss the weather, cricket score or the political scenario, and in all of this the manager is more than happy to put forth his opinions while the work gets done though perhaps a bit more leisurely than elsewhere.

The biggest draw of the small town remains its sense of quiet. After dark, I can still hear the crickets, spot a lone fox dancing as I walk back home, feel rather than see the mountains looming all around me and stop to listen to the nightjars or hear the sudden hoot of the owl.

But finally, wherever one lives, human nature remains constant. The kindnesses, the companionship and the fellow feeling can be found anywhere, as can cruelty, cunning and envy. It's what we look out for that we finally see in front of us.

Ruskin Bond

The Old Lama

I meet him on the road every morning, on my walk up to the Landour post office. He is a lean old man in a long maroon robe, a Tibetan monk of uncertain age. I'm told he's about 85. But age is really immaterial in the mountains. Some grow old at their mother's breasts, and there are others who do not age at all.

If you are like this old Lama, you go on forever. For he is a walking man, and there is no way you can stop him from walking.

Kim's Lama, rejuvenated by the mountain air, strode along with 'steady, driving strokes,' leaving his disciple far behind. My Lama, older and feebler than Kim's, walks very slowly, with the aid of an old walnut walking-stick. The ferrule keeps coming off the end of the stick, but lie puts it back with coal-tar left behind by the road repairers.

He plods and shuffles along. In fact, he is very like the tortoise in the story of the hare and the tortoise. I see him walking past my window, and five minutes later when I start out on the same road, I feel sure of overtaking him half way up the hill. But invariably I find him standing near the post-office when I get there.

He smiles when he sees me. We are always smiling at each other. His English is limited, and I have absolutely no Tibetan. He has a few words of Hindi, enough to make his needs known, but that is about all. He is quite happy to converse silently with all the creatures and people who take notice of him on the road.

It is the same walk he takes every morning. At nine o'clock, if I look out of my window, I can see a line of Tibetan prayer-flags fluttering over an old building in the cantonment. He emerges from beneath the flags and starts up the steep road. Ten minutes later he is below my window, and sometimes he stops to sit and rest on my steps, or on a parapet further along the road. Sooner or later, coming or going, I shall pass him on the road or up near the post-office. His eyes will twinkle behind thick-lensed glasses, and he will raise his walking-stick slightly in salutation. If I say something to him, he just smiles and nods vigorously in agreement.

An agreeable man. He was one of those who came to India in 1959, fleeing the Chinese occupation of Tibet. His Holiness the Dalai Lama found sanctuary in India, and lived in Mussoorie for a couple of years; many of his followers settled here. A new generation of Tibetans has grown up in the hill station, and those under 30 years have never seen their homeland. But for almost all of them—and there are several thousand in this district alone—Tibet is their country, their real home, and they are quick to express their determination to go back when their land is free again.

Even a twenty-year-old girl like Tseten, who has grown up knowing English and Hindi, speaks of the day when she will return to Tibet with her parents. She has given me a painting of

Milarepa, the Buddhist monk-philosopher, meditating beneath a fruit-laden peach tree, the eternal snows in the background. This is, perhaps, her vision of the Tibet she would like to see, some day. Meanwhile, she works as a typist in the office of the Tibetan Homes Foundation.

My old Lama will, I am sure, be among the first to return, even if he has to walk all the way, over the mountain passes. Maybe, that's why he plods up and around this hill every day. He is practising for the long walk back to Tibet. Here he is again, pausing at the foot of my steps. It's a cool, breezy morning, and he does not feel the need to sit down.

'Tashi-tilay!' (Good day!) I greet him, in the only Tibetan I know.

'Tashi-tilay!' he responds, beaming with delight.

'Will you go back to Tibet one day?' I ask him for the first time.

In spite of his limited Hindi, he understands me immediately, and nods vigorously.

'Soon, soon!' he exclaims, and raises his walking stick to emphasise, his words.

Yes, if the Tibetans are able to return to their country, he will be among the first to go back. His heart is still on that high plateau. And like the tortoise, he will be there waiting for the young hare to catch up with him.

If he goes, I shall certainly miss him on my walks.

The Long Day

Suraj was awakened by the sound of his mother busying herself in the kitchen. He lay in bed, looking through the open window at the sky getting lighter and the dawn pushing its way into the room. He knew there was something important about this new day, but for some time he couldn't remember what it was. Then, as the room cleared, his mind cleared. His school report would be arriving in the post.

Suraj knew he had failed. The class teacher had told him so. But his mother would only know of it when she read the report, and Suraj did not want to be in the house when she received it. He was sure it would be arriving today. So he had told his mother that he would be having his midday meal with his friend Somi—Somi, who wasn't even in town at the moment—and would be home only for the evening meal. By that time, he hoped, his mother would have recovered from the shock. He was glad his father was away on tour.

He slipped out of bed and went to the kitchen. His mother was surprised to see him up so early.

'I'm going for a walk, Ma,' he said, 'and then I'll go on to Somi's house.'

'Well, have your bath first and put something in your stomach.'

Suraj went to the tap in the courtyard and took a quick bath. He put on a clean shirt and shorts. Carelessly, he brushed his thick, curly hair, knowing he couldn't bring much order to its wildness. Then he gulped down a glass of milk and hurried out of the house. The postman wouldn't arrive for a couple of hours, but Suraj felt that the earlier his start the better. His mother was surprised and pleased to see him up and about so early.

Suraj was out on the maidaan and still the sun had not risen. The maidaan was an open area of grass, about a hundred square metres, and from the middle of it could be seen the mountains, range upon range of them, stepping into the sky. A game of football was in progress, and one of the players called out to Suraj to join them. Suraj said he wouldn't play for more than ten minutes, because he had some business to attend to; he kicked off his chappals and ran barefoot after the ball. Everyone was playing barefoot. It was an informal game, and the players were of all ages and sizes, from bearded Sikhs to small boys of six or seven. Suraj ran all over the place without actually getting in touch with the ball—he wasn't much good at football—and finally got into a scramble before the goal, fell and scratched his knee. He retired from the game even sooner than he had intended.

The scratch wasn't bad but there was some blood on his knee. He wiped it clean with his handkerchief and limped off the maidaan. He went in the direction of the railway station, but not through the bazaar. He went by way of the canal, which came from the foot of the nearest mountain, flowed through the town and down to the river. Beside the canal were the washerwomen, scrubbing and beating out clothes on the stone banks.

The canal was only a metre wide but, due to recent rain, the current was swift and noisy. Suraj stood on the bank, watching the rush of water. There was an inlet at one place, and here some children were bathing, and some were rushing up and down the bank, wearing nothing at all, shouting to each other in high spirits. Suraj felt like taking a dip too, but he did not know any of the children here; most of them were from very poor families. Hands in pockets, he walked along the canal banks.

The sun had risen and was pouring through the branches of the trees that lined the road. The leaves made shadowy patterns on the ground. Suraj tried hard not to think of his school report, but he knew that at any moment now the postman would be handing over a long brown envelope to his mother. He tried to imagine his mother's expression when she read the report; but the more he tried to picture her face, the more certain he was that, on knowing his result, she would show no expression at all. And having no expression on her face was much worse than having one.

Suraj heard the whistle of a train, and knew he was not far from the station. He cut through a field, climbed a hillock and ran down the slope until he was near the railway tracks. Here came the train, screeching and puffing: in the distance, a big black beetle, and then, when the carriages swung into sight, a centipede.

Suraj stood a good twenty metres away from the lines, on the slope of the hill. As the train passed, he pulled the handkerchief off his knee and began to wave it furiously. There was something about passing trains that filled him with awe and excitement. All those passengers, with mysterious lives and mysterious destinations, were people he wanted to know, people whose mysteries he wanted to unfold. He had been in a train recently, when his parents had taken him to bathe in the sacred river, Ganga, at Haridwar. He wished he could be in a train now; or, better still, be an engine-driver, with no more books and teachers and school reports. He did not know of any thirteen-year-old engine-drivers, but he saw himself driving the engine, shouting orders to the stoker; it made him feel powerful to be in control of a mighty steam-engine.

Someone—another boy—returned his wave, and the two waved at each other for a few seconds, and then the train had passed, its smoke spiralling backwards.

Suraj felt a little lonely now. Somehow, the passing of the train left him with a feeling of being alone in a wide, empty world. He was feeling hungry too. He went back to the field where he had seen some lichi trees, climbed into one of them and began plucking and peeling and eating the juicy red-skinned fruit. No one seemed to own the lichi trees because, although a dog appeared below and began barking, no one else appeared. Suraj kept spitting lichi seeds at the dog, and the dog kept barking at him. Eventually, the dog lost interest and slunk off.

Suraj began to feel drowsy in the afternoon heat. The lichi trees offered a lot of shade below, so he came down from the tree and sat on the grass, his back resting against the tree-trunk. A mynah-bird came hopping up to his feet and looked at him curiously, its head to one side.

Insects kept buzzing around Suraj. He swiped at them once or twice, but then couldn't make the effort to keep swiping. He opened his shirt buttons. The air was very hot, very still; the only sound was the faint buzzing of the insects. His head fell forward on his chest.

He opened his eyes to find himself being shaken, and looked up into the round, cheerful face of his friend Ranji.

'What are you doing, sleeping here?' asked Ranji, who was a couple of years younger than Suraj. 'Have you run away from home?'

'Not yet,' said Suraj. 'And what are you doing here?'

'Came for lichis.'

'So did I.'

They sat together for a while and talked and ate lichis. Then Ranji suggested that they visit the bazaar to eat fried pakoras.

'I haven't any money,' said Suraj.

'That doesn't matter,' said Ranji, who always seemed to be in funds. 'I have two rupees.'

So they walked to the bazaar. They crossed the field, walked back past the canal, skirted the maidaan, came to the clock tower and entered the bazaar.

The evening crowd had just begun to fill the road, and there was a lot of bustle and noise: the street-vendors called their wares in high, strident voices; children shouted and women bargained. There was a medley of smells and aromas coming from the little restaurants and sweet shops, and a medley of colours in the bangle and kite shops. Suraj and Ranji ate their pakoras, felt thirsty, and gazed at the rows and rows of coloured bottles at the cold drinks shop, where at least ten varieties of sweet, sticky, fizzy drinks were available. But they had already finished the two rupees, so there was nothing for them to do but quench their thirst at the municipal tap.

Afterwards they wandered down the crowded street, examining the shop-fronts, commenting on the passers-by, and every now and then greeting some friend or acquaintance. Darkness came on suddenly, and then the bazaar was lit up, the big shops with bright electric and neon lights, the street-vendors with oil-lamps. The bazaar at night was even more exciting than during the day.

They traversed the bazaar from end to end, and when they were at the clock tower again, Ranji said he had to go home, and left Suraj. It was nearing Suraj's dinnertime and so, unwillingly, he too turned homewards. He did not want it to appear that he was deliberately staying out late because of the school report.

The lights were on in the front room when he got home. He waited outside, secure in the darkness of the verandah, watching the lighted room. His mother would be waiting for him, she would probably have the report in her hand or on the kitchen shelf, and she would have lots and lots of questions to ask him.

All the cares of the world seemed to descend on Suraj as he crept into the house.

'You're late,' said his mother. 'Come and have your food.'

Suraj said nothing, but removed his shoes outside the kitchen and sat down cross-legged on the kitchen floor, which was where he took his meals. He was tired and hungry. He no longer cared about anything.

'One of your class-fellows dropped in,' said his mother. 'He said your reports were sent out today. They'll arrive tomorrow.'

Tomorrow! Suraj felt a great surge of relief.

But then, just as suddenly, his spirits fell again.

Tomorrow...a further postponement of the dread moment, another night and another morning something would have to be done about it!

'Ma,' he said abruptly. 'Somi has asked me to his house again tomorrow.'

'I don't know how his mother puts up with you so often,' said Suraj's mother.

Suraj lay awake in bed, planning the morrow's activities: a game of cricket or football on the maidaan; perhaps a dip in the canal; a half-hour watching the trains thunder past; and in the evening an hour in the bazaar, among the kites and balloons and rose-coloured fizzy drinks and round dripping syrupy sweets... Perhaps, in the morning, he could persuade his mother to give him two or three rupees... It would be his last rupees for quite some time.

Home

'The boy's useless,' said Mr Kapoor, speaking to his wife but making sure his son could hear. 'I don't know what he'll do with himself when he grows up. He takes no interest in his studies.'

Suraj's father had returned from a business trip and was seeing his son's school report for the first time. 'Good at cricket,' said the report. 'Poor in studies. Does not pay attention in class.'

Suraj's mother, a quiet, dignified woman, said nothing. Suraj stood at the window, refusing to speak. He stared out at the light drizzle that whispered across the garden. He had angry black eyes and bushy eyebrows, and he was feeling rebellious.

His father was doing all the talking. 'What's the use of spending money on his education if he can't show anything for it? He comes home, eats as much as three boys, asks for money, and then goes out to loaf with his friends!'

Mr Kapoor paused, expecting Suraj to reply and give cause for further scolding; but Suraj knew that silence would irritate his father even more, and there were times when he enjoyed watching his father get irritated.

'Well, I won't stand for it,' said Mr Kapoor finally. 'If you don't make some effort, my boy, you can leave this house!'

And having at last addressed Suraj directly, he stormed out of the room.

Suraj remained a few moments at the window. Then he went to the front door, opened it, stepped out into the rain, and banged the door behind him.

His mother made as if to call out after him, but she thought better of it, and turned and walked into the kitchen.

Suraj stood in the drizzle, looking back at the house.

'I'll never go back,' he said fiercely. 'I can manage without them. If they want me back, they can come and ask me to return!'

And he thrust his hands into his pockets and walked down the road with an independent air.

His fingers came into contact with a familiar crispness, a five rupee note. It was all the money he had in the world. He clutched it tight. He had meant to spend it at the cinema, but now it would have to serve more urgent needs. He wasn't sure what these needs would be because just now he was angry and his mind wasn't running on practical lines. He walked blindly, unconscious of the rain, until he reached the maidaan.

When he reached the maidaan, the sun came out.

Though there was still a drizzle, the sun seemed to raise Suraj's spirits at once. He remembered his friend Ranji and decided he would stay with Ranji until he found some sort of work. He knew that if he didn't find work, he wouldn't be able to stay away from home for long. He wondered what kind of work a thirteen-year-old could get. He did not fancy delivering newspapers or serving tea in a small tea shop in the bazaar; it was much better being a customer.

The drizzle ceased altogether, and Suraj hurried across the maidaan and down a quiet road until he reached Ranji's house. When he went in at the gate, his spirits sank.

The house was shut. There was a lock on the front door. Suraj went round the house three times but he couldn't find an open door or window. Perhaps, he thought, the family have gone out for the morning—a picnic or birthday treat; they were sure to be back for lunch. With spirits mounting once again, he strolled leisurely down the road, in the direction of the bazaar.

Suraj had a weakness for the bazaar, for its crowded variety of goods, its smells and colours and the music playing over the loudspeakers. He lingered now at a tea-and-pakora shop, tempted by the appetizing smells that came from inside; but decided that he would eat at Ranji's house and spend his money on something other than food. He couldn't resist the big yellow yo-yo in the toy-seller's glass case; it was set with pieces of different shine, coloured glass which shone and twinkled in the sunshine.

'How much?' asked Suraj.

'Two rupees,' said the shop-keeper. 'But to a regular customer like you I give it for one rupee.'

'It must be an old one,' said Suraj, but he paid the rupee and took possession of the yo-yo. He immediately began working it, strolling through the bazaar with the yo-yo swinging up and down from his index finger.

Fingering the four remaining notes in his pocket, he decided that he was thirsty. Not tap-water, nor a fizzy drink, but only a vanilla milkshake would meet his need. He sat at a table and sucked milkshake through a straw. One eye caught sight of the clock on the wall. It was nearly one o'clock. Ranji and his family should be home by now.

Suraj slipped off his chair, paid for the drink—that left him with two rupees—and went sauntering down the bazaar road, the yo-yo making soothing sounds beside him.

Ranji's house was still shut.

This was something Suraj hadn't anticipated. He walked quickly round the house, but it was locked as before. On his second round he met the gardener, an old man over sixty.

'Where is everybody?' asked Suraj.

'They have gone to Delhi for a week,' said the gardener, looking sharply at Suraj. 'Why, is anything the matter?'

Suraj had never seen the old man before, but he did not hesitate to confide in him. 'I've left home. I was going to stay with Ranji. Now there's nowhere to go.'

The old man thought this over for a minute. His face was wrinkled like a walnut, his hands and feet hard and cracked; but his eyes were bright and almost youthful.

He was a part-time gardener, who worked for several families along the road; there were no big gardens in this part of the town.

'Why don't you go home again?' he suggested.

'It's too soon,' said Suraj. 'I haven't really run away as yet. They must know I've run away. Then they'll feel sorry!'

The gardener smiled. 'You should have planned it better,' he said. 'Have you saved any money?' 'I had five rupees this morning. Now there are two rupees left.' He looked down at his yo-yo. 'Would you like to buy it?'

'I wouldn't know how to work it,' said the gardener. 'The

best thing for you to do is to go home, wait till Ranji gets back, and then run away.'

Suraj considered this interesting advice, and decided that there was something in it. But he didn't make up his mind right away. A little suspense at home would be a good thing for his parents.

He returned to the maidaan and sat down on the grass. As soon as he sat down, he felt hungry.

He had never felt so hungry before. Visions of tandoori chickens and dripping spangled sweets danced before him. He wondered if the toy-seller would take back the yo-yo. He probably would, for half the price; but, as much as Suraj wanted food, he did not want to give up the yo-yo.

There was nothing to do but go home. His mother, he was sure, would be worried by now. His father (he hoped) would be pacing up and down the verandah, glancing at his watch every few seconds. It would be a lesson to them. He would walk back into the house as if doing them a favour.

He only hoped they had kept his lunch.

Suraj walked into the sitting-room and threw his yoyo on the sofa.

Mr Kapoor was sitting in his favourite armchair, reading a newspaper prior to going back to his office. He stood up for a moment as Suraj came into the room, said 'You're very late,' and returned to his newspaper.

Suraj found his mother and his food in the kitchen. She did not speak to him, but was smiling to herself.

'Feeling hungry?' she asked.

'No,' said Suraj, and seized the tray and tucked into his food.

When he returned to the sitting-room he was surprised to see his father fumbling with the yo-yo.

'How do you work this stupid thing?' said Mr Kapoor.

Suraj didn't reply. He just stood there gloating over his father's clumsiness. At last he couldn't help bursting into laughter.

'It's easy,' he said. 'I'll show you.' And he took the yo-yo from his father and gave a demonstration.

When Mrs Kapoor came into the room she did not appear at all surprised to find her husband and son deeply absorbed in the working of a cheap bazaar toy. She was used to such absurdities. Men never really grew up.

Mr Kapoor had forgotten he was supposed to be returning to his office, and Suraj had forgotten about running away. They had both forgotten the morning's unpleasantness. That had been a long, long time ago.

At the Bank

Yes, those monkeys are at the bank too. They are there before it opens, doing their best to damage the roof; and they are there when it closes, tearing up the geraniums so lovingly planted by the manager.

I am also there when it opens, having, as usual, run short over the weekend, with the result that all I have in my pocket is a damaged fifty rupee note which I have attempted to repair with Sellotape.

The bank opens promptly at 10 a.m. Unfortunately, it doesn't have any money. No, it has not collapsed like the old Mansaram Bank, for which Ganesh Saili still has his father's chequebook showing a balance of three hundred rupees in 1957; the taxi with the cash (which comes from the main branch) has been caught in a traffic jam due to an unprecedented influx of tourists. This happens occasionally, as there are only two ways in and out of Mussoorie and only one way to Char Dukan.

Anyway, I pass the time by having a cup of tea with the manager and discussing the latest cricket test match with the cashier.

He is of the opinion that the result of a match depends on who wins the toss, while I maintain that the game is won by the team that has slept better the night before.

The cash arrives safely and I emerge into the sunshine to be met by several small boys who demand money for a cricket ball. I part with a new fifty rupee note (the old one having been obligingly changed by the cashier) and then run into several members of Tom Alter's cricket team, who insist that I join their Invitation XI in a game against the Dhobi Ghat Team, about to be played up at Chey-Tanki flat. (This was before the area got fenced off by the Defence establishment as cricket balls kept sailing into their offices and smashing their computers.)

Forgetting my age, but remembering my great days as a twelfth man for the Doon Heroes, I consented on condition that a substitute would field in my place. (No longer would I be a twelfth man.)

Well, the Dhobi Ghat Team put up a good score, and Tom's Invitation XI was trailing by some sixty or seventy runs, when I came in to bat at number seven. Tom was at the other end, holding the innings together.

The bowler (who ran a dry-cleaner's shop in town) was a real speedster, and his first ball caught me in the midriff. I am well padded there (by nature) but I resolved not to use that dry-cleaner's shop again. The second ball took the edge of my bat and sped away for four.

'Well played, Ruskin!' called Tom encouragingly, and I resolved to write a part for him in my next story.

I tapped the third ball into the covers and set off for a run, completely forgetting that I hadn't taken a run in fifty years. Still, I got to the other end, gasping for breath and trembling in the legs. Next, Tom tapped the ball away and called me for a run! There was no way I was going to join the brave souls sleeping in Jogger's Park (the name for the Landour cemetery), so I held up my hand and remained rooted to the crease. Tom was halfway down the pitch when the ball hit his stumps and he was run out. The look he gave me as he marched back to the pavilion was as effective as any that he had essayed in his more villainous roles.

I managed another streaky four before being bowled out, and when I returned to the 'pavilion' (the gardener's shed), Tom sportingly said, 'You should stick to writing, Ruskin'—quite forgetting that I had out-scored him!

After that, I had to pay for the refreshments and contribute towards the prize money (won by the Dhobi Ghat Team), and all this necessitated another trip to the bank before closing time. I was home well in time for lunch. My favourite rajma-bean curry with hot chapattis and mango pickle. As it was a Saturday, the kids were home from school, and we all tucked in—except for Gautam who was on a hunger-strike because his promised Saturday ice cream was missing. Then his father arrived and took us for a drive to Dhanaulti, where there was ice cream aplenty.

Gone are the days when a picnic involved preparing and packing a lunch basket, and then trudging off into the wilderness on a hot and dusty road. People don't walk anymore. They get into their cars and drive out to a crowded 'picnic spot' where dhabas will provide you with national dishes such as chowmein or pizzas. While Indian cuisine has taken over Britain, Chinese and Italian dishes have conquered Indian palates. That's globalization for you.

But I miss those picnics of old days. They were leisurely,

strung-out affairs. We seemed to have more time on our hands and a picnic meant an entire day's outing.

In Simla, we picnicked at the Brockhurst tennis courts (now apartment buildings), or out at Jutogh or Summer Hill, or beyond Chota Simla; but not at Jakko, where the monkeys—hundreds of them—were inclined to join in.

In Dehradun, we picnicked at Sulphur Springs, or in the hills near Rajpura, or on the banks of the Tons or Suswa rivers. You could also go fishing at Raiwala, just before the Song joins the Ganga. Equipped with rod and line, some friends and I went fishing there, but being inexperts, caught nothing. Some soldiers who were camping there had caught dozens of fish (by stunning them with explosives, I'm afraid) and were generous enough to give us a couple of large singharas. We returned to Dehra with our 'catch', and impressed friends and neighbours with our prowess as anglers.

Here in Mussoorie there was Mossy Falls, the Company Bagh, Clouds End, Haunted Houses and the banks of the little Aglar river.

I won't go down to the Aglar again, at least not on foot. Climbing up, ascending from 2,000 to 7,000 feet within a distance of three or four miles takes it out of you. On my first visit, some thirty years ago, I was accompanied by several school children. On our way back, we took the wrong path and lost our way (a frequent occurrence when I'm put in charge), and it was past ten o'clock when we were located by a bunch of anxious and angry parents accompanied by villagers who'd seen me going down. Fortunately, there was a full moon and there were no mishaps on the steep and stony path.

We went to bed hungry that night.

On another occasion, well provisioned with parathas, various sabzi, pickles, boiled eggs and bananas, two young friends—Kuku and Deepak—and I, tramped down to the Aglar and spread ourselves out on a grassy knoll. A pool of limpid water looked cool and inviting. We removed our clothes and plunged into the water. Great fun! We romped about, quite oblivious to what might be happening to our provisions. Then one of us looked up and yelled, 'Monkeys!' At least six of them were tucking into our lunch. We scrambled up the bank, and the monkeys fled, taking with them the remains of the parathas, the last bananas, and most of our underwear. They had left the pickle for us.

We were a sorry looking threesome by the time we returned to the town. But we did not go to bed hungry. We had enough money between us for a meal at Neelam's—the then most popular restaurant on the Mall—and we did full justice to various kababs, koftas, tikkas and tandoori rotis.

◆

By now my readers will have come to the conclusion that I am perpetually persecuted by monkeys. And you would not be far wrong, gentle reader. Even as I write, I see one grinning at me from my window. Fortunately the window is closed and he cannot get in. I stick my tongue out at him, and he takes off, finding me far more hideous than his friends and relations. But it wasn't always like that. Some years ago, when I lived in Maplewood, on the edge of the forest, a little girl monkey would sometimes perch shyly on the windowsill and study me with friendly curiosity. The rest of her tribe showed no interest in me as a person, but this little girl—and I think of her as a human rather than as a monkey—would turn up every morning while I was at my typewriter, and sit there quietly, her eyes intent on me as I tapped out a story or article. Perhaps it was the typewriter that fascinated her. I like to think it was my blue eyes. She had blue eyes too!

Now it isn't often that girls take a fancy to me, but I like to think that the little monkey had a crush on me. Her eyes had a gentle, appealing look, and she would make little chuckling sounds that I took for intimate conversation. If I approached, she would leap onto the walnut tree just outside the window and gesture to me to join her there. But my tree-climbing days were already over; and besides, I was afraid of her peers and parents.

One day I came into the room and found her at the typewriter, playing with the keys. When she saw me, she returned to the window and looked guilty. I looked down at the sheet in my machine. Had she been trying to give me a message? It read something like this—*!;!_1;:0—and there it broke off. I'm convinced she was trying to write the word 'love'.

However, I never did find out for sure, and the tribe went away, taking my girl friend with them. I never saw her again. Perhaps they married her off.

◆

Talking of marriages, I am often asked by sympathetic readers why I never married. Now that's a long, sad story which would be out of place here, but I can tell you the story of my Uncle

Bertie and why he never married.

As a young man, Uncle Bertie worked at the Ishapore rifle factory, which is just outside Kolkata. In pre-Independence days, Ishapore had a large Anglo-Indian and European community, many of whom were employed in the factory. Uncle Bertie was an impetuous fellow. He had a bit of a fling with a girl who lived across the road, and after a romp in the nearest mango-grove, he asked her to marry him. She agreed with alacrity. She was older than him, much taller, and her figure—46, 46, 46—would have been the envy of Marlene Dietrich or Marilyn Monroe. The girl's parents were agreeable, and everything had been arranged when Bertie Bond began to have second thoughts. He was always one for second thoughts. His brief infatuation over, he began to wonder what he had seen in the girl in the first place. She liked going to dances and Bertie couldn't dance. Her reading was limited to film magazines such as *Hollywood Romance*, while Bertie read Maxim Gorky and Emile Zola. She could not cook. Nor could Bertie. And khansamas were expensive. She liked to go shopping and Bertie's salary was three hundred rupees per month.

The banns were announced, the great day came around, and the church filled up with friends, relatives and well-wishers. The padre put on his gown and prepared to take the wedding service. The bride was present, arrayed in the white wedding dress in which her mother had been married. But there was no sign of Bertie. Half an hour, an hour, two hours passed. The bridegroom could not be found.

He had, in fact, fled to Calcutta, and had gone underground. He remained underground for sometime, emerging from hiding only in order to take a job at the docks in Ishapore. Everyone was waiting for him to return. They had varied and interesting ideas of what they would do to him. Some of them are still waiting.

'Marriage,' said Oscar Wilde, 'is a romance in which the hero dies in the first chapter.'

Uncle Bertie made his exit in the preface.

Monkey Trouble

Grandfather bought Tutu from a street entertainer for the sum of ten rupees. The man had three monkeys. Tutu was the smallest, but the most mischievous. She was tied up most of the time. The little monkey looked so miserable with a collar and chain that Grandfather decided it would be much happier in our home. Grandfather had a weakness for keeping unusual pets. It was a habit that I, at the age of eight or nine, used to encourage.

Grandmother at first objected to having a monkey in the house. 'You have enough pets as it is,' she said, referring to Grandfather's goat, several white mice, and a small tortoise.

'But I don't have any,' I said.

'You're wicked enough for two monkeys. One boy in the house is all I can take.'

'Ah, but Tutu isn't a boy,' said Grandfather triumphantly. 'This is a little girl monkey!'

Grandmother gave in. She had always wanted a little girl in the house. She believed girls were less troublesome than boys. Tutu was to prove her wrong.

She was a pretty little monkey. Her bright eyes sparkled with mischief beneath deep-set eyebrows. And her teeth, which were a pearly white, were often revealed in a grin that frightened the wits out of Aunt Ruby, whose nerves had already suffered from the presence of Grandfather's pet python. But this was my grandparents' house, and aunts and uncles had to put up with our pets.

Tutu's hands had a dried-up look, as though they had been pickled in the sun for many years. One of the first things I taught her was to shake hands, and this she insisted on doing with all who visited the house. Peppery Major Malik would have to stoop and shake hands with Tutu before he could enter the drawing room, otherwise Tutu would climb onto his shoulder and stay there, roughing up his hair and playing with his moustache.

Uncle Benji couldn't stand any of our pets and took a particular dislike to Tutu, who was always making faces at him. But as Uncle Benji was never in a job for long, and depended on Grandfather's good-natured generosity, he had to shake hands with Tutu, like everyone else.

Tutu's fingers were quick and wicked. And her tail, while adding to her good looks (Grandfather believed a tail would add to anyone's good looks!), also served as a third hand. She could use it to hang from a branch, and it was capable of scooping up any delicacy that might be out of reach of her hands.

On one of Aunt Ruby's visits, loud shrieks from her bedroom brought us running to see what was wrong. It was only Tutu trying on Aunt Ruby's petticoats! They were much too large, of course, and when Aunt Ruby entered the room, all she saw was a faceless white blob jumping up and down on the bed.

We disentangled Tutu and soothed Aunt Ruby. I gave Tutu

a bunch of sweet peas to make her happy. Granny didn't like anyone plucking her sweet peas, so I took some from Major Malik's garden while he was having his afternoon siesta.

Then Uncle Benji complained that his hairbrush was missing. We found Tutu sunning herself on the back verandah, using the hairbrush to scratch her armpits.

I took it from her and handed it back to Uncle Benji with an apology; but he flung the brush away with an oath.

'Such a fuss about nothing,' I said. 'Tutu doesn't have fleas!'

'No, and she bathes more often than Benji,' said Grandfather, who had borrowed Aunt Ruby's shampoo to give Tutu a bath.

All the same, Grandmother objected to Tutu being given the run of the house. Tutu had to spend her nights in the outhouse, in the company of the goat. They got on quite well, and it was not long before Tutu was seen sitting comfortably on the back of the goat, while the goat roamed the back garden in search of its favourite grass.

The day Grandfather had to visit Meerut to collect his railway pension, he decided to take Tutu and me along to keep us both out of mischief, he said. To prevent Tutu from wandering about on the train, causing inconvenience to other passengers, she was provided with a large black travelling bag. This, with some straw at the bottom, became her compartment. Grandfather and I paid for our seats, and we took Tutu along as hand baggage.

There was enough space for Tutu to look out of the bag occasionally, and to be fed with bananas and biscuits, but she could not get her hands through the opening and the canvas was too strong for her to bite her way through.

Tutu's efforts to get out only had the effect of making the bag roll about on the floor or occasionally jump into the air—an exhibition that attracted a curious crowd of onlookers at the Dehra and Meerut railway stations.

Anyway, Tutu remained in the bag as far as Meerut, but while Grandfather was producing our tickets at the turnstile, she suddenly poked her head out of the bag and gave the ticket collector a wide grin.

The poor man was taken aback. But, with a great presence of mind and much to Grandfather's annoyance, he said, 'Sir, you have a dog with you. You'll have to buy a ticket for it.'

'It's not a dog!' said Grandfather indignantly. 'This is a baby monkey of the species *macacus mischievous*, closely related to the human species *homus horriblis*! And there is no charge for babies!'

'It's as big as a cat,' said the ticket collector. 'Cats and dogs have to be paid for.'

'But, I tell you, it's only a baby!' protested Grandfather.

'Have you a birth certificate to prove that?' demanded the ticket collector.

'Next, you'll be asking to see her mother,' snapped Grandfather.

In vain did he take Tutu out of the bag. In vain did he try to prove that a young monkey did not qualify as a dog or a cat or even as a quadruped. Tutu was classified as a dog by the ticket collector, and five rupees were handed over as her fare.

Then Grandfather, just to get his own back, took from his pocket the small tortoise that he sometimes carried about, and said: 'And what must I pay for this, since you charge for all creatures great and small?'

The ticket collector looked closely at the tortoise, prodded it with his forefinger, gave Grandfather a triumphant look, and said, 'No charge, sir. It is not a dog!'

Winters in North India can be very cold. A great treat for Tutu on winter evenings was the large bowl of hot water given to her by Grandfather for a bath. Tutu would cunningly test the temperature with her hand, then gradually step into the bath, first one foot, then the other (as she had seen me doing) until she was in the water upto her neck.

Once comfortable, she would take the soap in her hands or feet and rub herself all over. When the water became cold, she would get out and run as quickly as she could to the kitchen fire in order to dry herself. If anyone laughed at her during this performance, Tutu's feelings would be hurt and she would refuse to go on with the bath.

One day, Tutu almost succeeded in boiling herself alive. Grandmother had left a large kettle on the fire for tea. And Tutu, all by herself and with nothing better to do, decided to remove the lid. Finding the water just warm enough for a bath, she got in, with her head sticking out from the open kettle.

This was fine for a while, until the water began to get heated. Tutu raised herself a little. But finding it cold outside, she sat down again. She continued hopping up and down for some time, until Grandmother returned and hauled her, half-boiled, out of the kettle.

'What's for tea today?' asked Uncle Benji gleefully. 'Boiled eggs and a half-boiled monkey?'

But Tutu was none the worse for the adventure and continued to bathe more regularly than Uncle Benji.

Aunt Ruby was a frequent taker of baths. This met with Tutu's approval—so much so that, one day, when Aunt Ruby had finished shampooing her hair, she looked up through a lather of bubbles and soap suds to see Tutu sitting opposite her in the bath, following her example.

One day Aunt Ruby took us all by surprise. She announced that she had become engaged. We had always thought Aunt Ruby would never marry—she had often said so herself—but it appeared that the right man had now come along in the person of Rocky Fernandes, a schoolteacher from Goa.

Rocky was a tall, firm-jawed, good-natured man, a couple of years younger than Aunt Ruby. He had a fine baritone voice and sang in the manner of the great Nelson Eddy. As Grandmother liked baritone singers, Rocky was soon in her good books.

'But what on earth does he see in her?' Uncle Benji wanted to know.

'More than any girl has seen in you!' snapped Grandmother. 'Ruby's a fine girl. And they're both teachers. Maybe they can start a school of their own.'

Rocky visited the house quite often and brought me chocolates and cashew nuts, of which he seemed to have an unlimited supply. He also taught me several marching songs. Naturally, I approved of Rocky. Aunt Ruby won my grudging admiration for having made such a wise choice.

One day, I overheard them talking of going to the bazaar to buy an engagement ring. I decided I would go along, too. But as Aunt Ruby had made it clear that she did not want me around, I decided that I had better follow at a discreet distance. Tutu, becoming aware that a mission of some importance was under way, decided to follow me. But as I had not invited her along, she too decided to keep out of sight.

Once in the crowded bazaar, I was able to get quite close to Aunt Ruby and Rocky without being spotted. I waited until they had settled down in a large jewellery shop before sauntering past and spotting them, as though by accident. Aunt Ruby wasn't too pleased at seeing me, but Rocky waved and called out, 'Come and join us! Help your aunt choose a beautiful ring!'

The whole thing seemed to be a waste of good money, but I did not say so—Aunt Ruby was giving me one of her more unloving looks.

'Look, these are pretty!' I said, pointing to some cheap, bright agates set in white metal. But Aunt Ruby wasn't looking. She was immersed in a case of diamonds.

'Why not a ruby for Aunt Ruby?' I suggested, trying to please her.

'That's her lucky stone,' said Rocky. 'Diamonds are the thing for engagements.' And he started singing a song about a diamond being a girl's best friend.

While the jeweller and Aunt Ruby were sifting through the diamond rings, and Rocky was trying out another tune, Tutu had slipped into the shop without being noticed by anyone but me. A little squeal of delight was the first sign she gave of her presence. Everyone looked up to see her trying on a pretty necklace.

'And what are those stones?' I asked.

'They look like pearls,' said Rocky.

'They *are* pearls,' said the shopkeeper, making a grab for them.

'It's that dreadful monkey!' cried Aunt Ruby. 'I knew that boy would bring him here!'

The necklace was already adorning Tutu's neck. I thought she looked rather nice in pearls, but she gave us no time to admire the effect. Springing out of our reach, Tutu dodged around Rocky, slipped between my legs, and made for the crowded road. I ran after her, shouting out to her to stop, but she wasn't listening.

There were no branches to assist Tutu in her progress, but she used the heads and shoulders of people as springboards and so made rapid headway through the bazaar.

The jeweller left his shop and ran after us. So did Rocky. So did several bystanders who had seen the incident. And others, who had no idea what it was all about, joined in the chase. As Grandfather used to say, 'In a crowd, everyone plays follow-the-leader, even when they don't know who's leading.' Not everyone knew that the leader was Tutu. Only the front runners could see her.

She tried to make her escape speedier by leaping onto the back of a passing scooterist. The scooter swerved into a fruit stall and came to a standstill under a heap of bananas, while the scooterist found himself in the arms of an indignant fruitseller. Tutu peeled a banana and ate part of it, before deciding to move on.

From an awning, she made an emergency landing on a washerman's donkey. The donkey promptly panicked and rushed down the road, while bundles of washing fell by the wayside. The washerman joined in the chase. Children on their way to school decided that there was something better to do than attend classes. With shouts of glee, they soon overtook their panting elders.

Tutu finally left the bazaar and took a road leading in the direction of our house. But knowing that she would be caught and locked up once she got home, she decided to end the chase by ridding herself of the necklace. Deftly removing it from her neck, she flung it in the small canal that ran down the road.

The jeweller, with a cry of anguish, plunged into the canal. So did Rocky. So did I. So did several other people, both adults and children. It was to be a treasure hunt!

Some twenty minutes later, Rocky shouted, 'I've found it!' Covered in mud, water lilies, ferns and tadpoles, we emerged from the canal, and Rocky presented the necklace to the relieved shopkeeper.

Everyone trudged back to the bazaar to find Aunt Ruby waiting in the shop, still trying to make up her mind about a suitable engagement ring.

Finally the ring was bought, the engagement was announced, and a date was set for the wedding.

'I don't want that monkey anywhere near us on our wedding day,' declared Aunt Ruby.

'We'll lock her up in the outhouse,' promised Grandfather. 'And we'll let her out only after you've left for your honeymoon.'

A few days before the wedding I found Tutu in the kitchen, helping Grandmother prepare the wedding cake. Tutu often helped with the cooking and, when Grandmother wasn't looking, added herbs, spices, and other interesting items to the pots—so that occasionally we found a chilli in the custard or an onion in the jelly or a strawberry floating in the chicken soup.

Sometimes these additions improved a dish, sometimes they did not. Uncle Benji lost a tooth when he bit firmly into a sandwich which contained walnut shells.

I'm not sure exactly what went into that wedding cake when Grandmother wasn't looking—she insisted that Tutu was always very well-behaved in the kitchen—but I did spot Tutu stirring in some red chilli sauce, bitter gourd seeds, and a generous helping of egg shells!

It's true that some of the guests were not seen for several days after the wedding, but no one said anything against the cake. Most people thought it had an interesting flavour.

The great day dawned, and the wedding guests made their way to the little church that stood on the outskirts of Dehra—a town with a church, two mosques, and several temples.

I had offered to dress Tutu up as a bridesmaid and bring her along, but no one except Grandfather thought it was a good idea. So I was an obedient boy and locked Tutu in the outhouse. I did, however, leave the skylight open a little. Grandmother had always said that fresh air was good for growing children, and I thought Tutu should have her share of it.

The wedding ceremony went without a hitch. Aunt Ruby looked a picture, and Rocky looked like a film star.

Grandfather played the organ, and did so with such gusto that the small choir could hardly be heard. Grandmother cried a little. I sat quietly in a corner, with the little tortoise on my lap.

When the service was over, we trooped out into the sunshine and made our way back to the house for the reception.

The feast had been laid out on tables in the garden. As the gardener had been left in charge, everything was in order.

Tutu was on her best behaviour. She had, it appeared, used the skylight to avail of more fresh air outside, and now sat beside the three-tier wedding cake, guarding it against crows, squirrels and the goat. She greeted the guests with squeals of delight.

It was too much for Aunt Ruby. She flew at Tutu in a rage. And Tutu, sensing that she was not welcome, leapt away, taking with her the top tier of the wedding cake.

Led by Major Malik, we followed her into the orchard, only to find that she had climbed to the top of the jackfruit tree. From there she proceeded to pelt us with bits of wedding cake. She had also managed to get hold of a bag of confetti, and when she ran out of cake she showered us with confetti.

'That's more like it!' said the good-humoured Rocky. 'Now let's return to the party, folks!'

Uncle Benji remained with Major Malik, determined to chase Tutu away. He kept throwing stones into the tree, until he received a large piece of cake bang on his nose. Muttering threats, he returned to the party, leaving the Major to carry on the battle.

When the festivities were finally over, Uncle Benji took the old car out of the garage and drove up the verandah steps. He was going to drive Aunt Ruby and Rocky to the nearby hill resort of Mussoorie, where they would have their honeymoon.

Watched by family and friends, Aunt Ruby climbed into the back seat. She waved regally to everyone. She leant out of the window and offered me her cheek and I had to kiss her farewell. Everyone wished them luck.

As Rocky burst into a song, Uncle Benji opened the throttle and stepped on the accelerator. The car shot forward in a cloud of dust.

Rocky and Aunt Ruby continued to wave at us. And so did Tutu, from her perch on the rear bumper! She was clutching a bag in her hands and showering confetti on all who stood in the driveway.

'They don't know Tutu's with them!' I exclaimed. 'She'll go all the way to Mussoorie! Will Aunt Ruby let her stay with them?'

'Tutu might ruin the honeymoon,' said Grandfather. 'But don't worry—our Benji will bring her back!'

Snake Trouble

1

After retiring from the Indian Railways and settling in Dehra, Grandfather often made his days (and ours) more exciting by keeping unusual pets. He paid a snake charmer in the bazaar twenty rupees for a young python. Then, to the delight of a curious group of boys and girls, he slung the python over his shoulder and brought it home.

I was with him at the time, and felt very proud walking beside Grandfather. He was popular in Dehra, especially among the poorer people, and everyone greeted him politely without seeming to notice the python. They were, in fact, quite used to seeing him in the company of strange creatures.

The first to see us arrive was Tutu the monkey, who was swinging from a branch of the jackfruit tree. One look at the python, ancient enemy of her race, and she fled into the house squealing with fright. Then our parrot, Popeye, who had his perch on the verandah, set up the most awful shrieking and whistling. His whistle was like that of a steam engine. He had learnt to do this in earlier days, when we had lived near railway stations.

The noise brought Grandmother to the verandah, where she nearly fainted at the sight of the python curled round Grandfather's neck.

Grandmother put up with most of his pets, but she drew the line at reptiles. Even a sweet-tempered lizard made her blood run cold. There was little chance that she would allow a python in the house.

'It will strangle you to death!' she cried.

'Nonsense,' said Grandfather. 'He's only a young fellow.'

'He'll soon get used to us,' I added by way of support.

'He might, indeed,' said Grandmother, 'but I have no intention of getting used to him. And your Aunt Ruby is coming to stay with us tomorrow. She'll leave the minute she knows there's a snake in the house.'

'Well, perhaps we should show it to her first thing,' said Grandfather, who found Aunt Ruby rather tiresome.

'Get rid of it right away,' said Grandmother.

'I can't let it loose in the garden. It might find its way into the chicken shed, and then where will we be?'

'Minus a few chickens,' I said reasonably, but this only made Grandmother more determined to get rid of the python.

'Lock that awful thing in the bathroom,' she said. 'Go and find the man you bought it from, and get him to come here and collect it! He can keep the money you gave him.'

Grandfather and I took the snake into the bathroom and placed it in an empty tub. Looking a bit crestfallen, he said, 'Perhaps your grandmother is right. I'm not worried about Aunt Ruby, but we don't want the python to get hold of Tutu or Popeye.'

We hurried off to the bazaar in search of the snake charmer but hadn't gone far when we found several snake charmers looking for us. They had heard that Grandfather was buying snakes, and they had brought with them snakes of various sizes and descriptions.

'No, no!' protested Grandfather. 'We don't want more snakes. We want to return the one we bought.'

But the man who had sold it to us had, apparently, returned to his village in the jungle, looking for another python for Grandfather; and the other snake charmers were not interested in buying, only in selling. In order to shake them off, we had to return home by a roundabout route, climbing a wall and cutting through an orchard. We found Grandmother pacing up and down the verandah. One look at our faces and she knew we had failed to get rid of the snake.

'All right,' said Grandmother. 'Just take it away yourselves and see that it doesn't come back.'

'We'll get rid of it, Grandmother,' I said confidently. 'Don't you worry.'

Grandfather opened the bathroom door and stepped into the room. I was close behind him. We couldn't see the python anywhere.

'He's gone,' announced Grandfather.

'We left the window open,' I said.

'Deliberately, no doubt,' said Grandmother. 'But it couldn't have gone far. You'll have to search the grounds.'

A careful search was made of the house, the roof, the kitchen, the garden and the chicken shed, but there was no sign of the python.

'He must have gone over the garden wall,' Grandfather said cheerfully. 'He'll be well away by now!'

The python did not reappear, and when Aunt Ruby arrived with enough luggage to show that she had come for a long visit, there was only the parrot to greet her with a series of long, ear-splitting whistles.

2

For a couple of days Grandfather and I were a little worried that the python might make a sudden reappearance, but when he didn't show up again we felt he had gone for good. Aunt Ruby had to put up with Tutu the monkey making faces at her, something I did only when she wasn't looking; and she complained that Popeye shrieked loudest when she was in the room; but she was used to them, and knew she would have to bear with them if she was going to stay with us.

And then, one evening, we were startled by a scream from the garden.

Seconds later, Aunt Ruby came flying up the verandah steps, gasping, 'In the guava tree! I was reaching for a guava when I saw it staring at me. The look in its eyes! As though it would eat me alive—'

'Calm down, dear,' urged Grandmother, sprinkling rose water over my aunt. 'Tell us, what *did* you see?'

'A snake!' sobbed Aunt Ruby. 'A great boa constrictor in the guava tree. Its eyes were terrible, and it looked at me in such a queer way.'

'Trying to tempt you with a guava, no doubt,' said Grandfather, turning away to hide his smile. He gave me a look full of meaning, and I hurried out into the garden. But when I got to the guava tree, the python (if it had been the python) had gone.

'Aunt Ruby must have frightened it off,' I told Grandfather.

'I'm not surprised,' he said. 'But it will be back, Ranji. I think it has taken a fancy to your aunt.'

Sure enough, the python began to make brief but frequent appearances, usually up in the most unexpected places.

One morning I found him curled up on a dressing table, gazing at his own reflection in the mirror. I went for Grandfather, but by the time we returned the python had moved on.

He was seen again in the garden, and one day I spotted him climbing the iron ladder to the roof. I set off after him, and was soon up the ladder, which I had climbed up many times. I arrived on the flat roof just in time to see the snake disappearing down a drainpipe. The end of his tail was visible for a few moments and then that too disappeared.

'I think he lives in the drainpipe,' I told Grandfather.

'Where does it get its food?' asked Grandmother.

'Probably lives on those field rats that used to be such a nuisance. Remember, they lived in the drainpipes too.'

'Hmm...' Grandmother looked thoughtful. 'A snake has its uses. Well, as long as it keeps to the roof and prefers rats to chickens...'

But the python did not confine itself to the roof. Piercing shrieks from Aunt Ruby had us all rushing to her room. There was the python on *her* dressing table, apparently admiring himself in the mirror.

'All the attention he's been getting has probably made him

conceited,' said Grandfather, picking up the python to the accompaniment of further shrieks from Aunt Ruby. 'Would you like to hold him for a minute, Ruby? He seems to have taken a fancy to you.'

Aunt Ruby ran from the room and onto the verandah, where she was greeted with whistles of derision from Popeye the parrot. Poor Aunt Ruby! She cut short her stay by a week and returned to Lucknow, where she was a schoolteacher. She said she felt safer in her school than she did in our house.

3

Having seen Grandfather handle the python with such ease and confidence, I decided I would do likewise. So the next time I saw the snake climbing the ladder to the roof, I climbed up alongside him. He stopped, and I stopped too. I put out my hand, and he slid over my arm and up to my shoulder. As I did not want him coiling round my neck, I gripped him with both hands and carried him down to the garden. He didn't seem to mind.

The snake felt rather cold and slippery and at first he gave me goose pimples. But I soon got used to him, and he must have liked the way I handled him, because when I set him down he wanted to climb up my leg. As I had other things to do, I dropped him in a large empty basket that had been left out in the garden. He stared out at me with unblinking, expressionless eyes. There was no way of knowing what he was thinking, if indeed he thought at all.

I went off for a bicycle ride, and when I returned, I found Grandmother picking guavas and dropping them into the basket.

The python must have gone elsewhere.

When the basket was full, Grandmother said, 'Will you take these to Major Malik? It's his birthday and I want to give him a nice surprise.'

I fixed the basket on the carrier of my cycle and pedalled off to Major Malik's house at the end of the road. The major met me on the steps of his house.

'And what has your kind granny sent me today, Ranji?' he asked.

'A surprise for your birthday, sir,' I said, and put the basket down in front of him.

The python, who had been buried beneath all the guavas, chose this moment to wake up and stand straight up to a height of several feet. Guavas tumbled all over the place. The major uttered an oath and dashed indoors.

I pushed the python back into the basket, picked it up, mounted the bicycle, and rode out of the gate in record time. And it was as well that I did so, because Major Malik came charging out of the house armed with a double-barrelled shotgun, which he was waving all over the place.

'Did you deliver the guavas?' asked Grandmother when I got back.

'I delivered them,' I said truthfully.

'And was he pleased?'

'He's going to write and thank you,' I said.

And he did.

'Thank you for the lovely surprise,' he wrote. *'Obviously you could not have known that my doctor had advised me against any undue excitement. My blood pressure has been rather high. The sight*

of your grandson does not improve it. All the same, it's the thought that matters and I take it all in good humour…'

'What a strange letter,' said Grandmother. 'He must be ill, poor man. Are guavas bad for blood pressure?'

'Not by themselves, they aren't,' said Grandfather, who had an inkling of what had happened. 'But together with other things they can be a bit upsetting.'

4

Just when all of us, including Grandmother, were getting used to having the python about the house and grounds, it was decided that we would be going to Lucknow for a few months.

Lucknow was a large city, about three hundred miles from Dehra. Aunt Ruby lived and worked there. We would be staying with her, and so of course we couldn't take any pythons, monkeys or other unusual pets with us.

'What about Popeye?' I asked.

'Popeye isn't a pet,' said Grandmother. 'He's one of us. He comes too.'

And so the Dehra railway platform was thrown into confusion by the shrieks and whistles of our parrot, who could imitate both the guard's whistle and the whistle of a train. People dashed into their compartments, thinking the train was about to leave, only to realize that the guard hadn't blown his whistle after all. When they got down, Popeye would let out another shrill whistle, which sent everyone rushing for the train again. This happened several times until the guard actually blew his whistle. Then nobody bothered to get on, and several passengers were left behind.

'Can't you gag that parrot?' asked Grandfather, as the train moved out of the station and picked up speed.

'I'll do nothing of the sort,' said Grandmother. 'I've bought a ticket for him, and he's entitled to enjoy the journey as much as anyone.'

Whenever we stopped at a station, Popeye objected to fruit sellers and other people poking their heads in through the windows. Before the journey was over, he had nipped two fingers and a nose, and tweaked a ticket inspector's ear.

It was to be a night journey, and presently Grandmother covered herself with a blanket and stretched out on the berth. 'It's been a tiring day. I think I'll go to sleep,' she said.

'Aren't we going to eat anything?' I asked.

'I'm not hungry—I had something before we left the house. You two help yourselves from the picnic hamper.'

Grandmother dozed off, and even Popeye started nodding, lulled to sleep by the clackety-clack of the wheels and the steady puffing of the steam engine.

'Well, I'm hungry,' I said. 'What did Granny make for us?'

'Stuffed samosas, omelettes, and tandoori chicken. It's all in the hamper under the berth.'

I tugged at the cane box and dragged it into the middle of the compartment. The straps were loosely tied. No sooner had I undone them than the lid flew open, and I let out a gasp of surprise.

In the hamper was a python, curled up contentedly. There was no sign of our dinner.

'It's a python,' I said. 'And it's finished all our dinner.'

'Nonsense,' said Grandfather, joining me near the hamper.

'Pythons won't eat omelette and samosas. They like their food alive! Why, this isn't our hamper. The one with our food in it must have been left behind! Wasn't it Major Malik who helped us with our luggage? I think he's got his own back on us by changing the hamper!'

Grandfather snapped the hamper shut and pushed it back beneath the berth.

'Don't let Grandmother see him,' he said. 'She might think we brought him along on purpose.'

'Well, I'm hungry,' I complained.

'Wait till we get to the next station, then we can buy some pakoras. Meanwhile, try some of Popeye's green chillies.'

'No thanks,' I said. 'You have them, Grandad.'

And Grandfather, who could eat chillies plain, popped a couple into his mouth and munched away contentedly.

A little after midnight there was a great clamour at the end of the corridor. Popeye made complaining squawks, and Grandfather and I got up to see what was wrong.

Suddenly there were cries of 'Snake, snake!'

I looked under the berth. The hamper was open.

'The python's out,' I said, and Grandfather dashed out of the compartment in his pyjamas. I was close behind.

About a dozen passengers were bunched together outside the washroom.

'Anything wrong?' asked Grandfather casually.

'We can't get into the toilet,' said someone. 'There's a huge snake inside.'

'Let me take a look,' said Grandfather. 'I know all about snakes.'

The passengers made way, and Grandfather and I entered the washroom together, but there was no sign of the python.

'He must have got out through the ventilator,' said Grandfather. 'By now he'll be in another compartment!' Emerging from the washroom, he told the assembled passengers, 'It's gone! Nothing to worry about. Just a harmless young python.'

When we got back to our compartment, Grandmother was sitting up on her berth.

'I *knew* you'd do something foolish behind my back,' she scolded. 'You told me you'd left that creature behind, and all this time it was with us on the train.'

Grandfather tried to explain that we had nothing to do with it, that this python had been smuggled onto the train by Major Malik, but Grandmother was unconvinced.

'Anyway, it's gone,' said Grandfather. 'It must have fallen out of the washroom window. We're over a hundred miles from Dehra, so you'll never see it again.'

Even as he spoke, the train slowed down and lurched to a grinding halt.

'No station here,' said Grandfather, putting his head out of the window.

Someone came rushing along the embankment, waving his arms and shouting.

'I do believe it's the stoker,' said Grandfather. 'I'd better go and see what's wrong.'

'I'm coming too,' I said, and together we hurried along the length of the stationary train until we reached the engine.

'What's up?' called Grandfather. 'Anything I can do to help? I know all about engines.'

But the engine driver was speechless. And who could blame him? The python had curled itself about his legs, and the driver was too petrified to move.

'Just leave it to us,' said Grandfather, and, dragging the python off the driver, he dumped the snake in my arms. The engine driver sank down on the floor, pale and trembling.

'I think I'd better drive the engine,' said Grandfather. 'We don't want to be late getting into Lucknow. Your aunt will be expecting us!' And before the astonished driver could protest, Grandfather had released the brakes and set the engine in motion.

'We've left the stoker behind,' I said.

'Never mind. You can shovel the coal.'

Only too glad to help Grandfather drive an engine, I dropped the python in the driver's lap and started shovelling coal. The engine picked up speed and we were soon rushing through the darkness, sparks flying skywards and the steam whistle shrieking almost without pause.

'You're going too fast!' cried the driver.

'Making up for lost time,' said Grandfather. 'Why did the stoker run away?'

'He went for the guard. You've left them both behind!'

5

Early next morning, the train steamed safely into Lucknow. Explanations were in order, but as the Lucknow station master was an old friend of Grandfather's, all was well. We had arrived twenty minutes early, and while Grandfather went off to have a cup of tea with the engine driver and the station master, I returned the python to the hamper and helped Grandmother with the luggage. Popeye stayed perched on Grandmother's shoulder, eyeing the busy platform with deep distrust. He was the first to see Aunt Ruby striding down the platform, and let out a warning whistle.

Aunt Ruby, a lover of good food, immediately spotted the picnic hamper, picked it up and said, 'It's quite heavy. You must have kept something for me! I'll carry it out to the taxi.'

'We hardly ate anything,' I said.

'It seems ages since I tasted something cooked by your granny.' And after that there was no getting the hamper away from Aunt Ruby.

Glancing at it, I thought I saw the lid bulging, but I had tied it down quite firmly this time and there was little likelihood of its suddenly bursting open.

Grandfather joined us outside the station and we were soon settled inside the taxi. Aunt Ruby gave instructions to the driver and we shot off in a cloud of dust.

'I'm dying to see what's in the hamper,' said Aunt Ruby. 'Can't I take just a little peek?'

'Not now,' said Grandfather. 'First let's enjoy the breakfast you've got waiting for us.'

Popeye, perched proudly on Grandmother's shoulder, kept one suspicious eye on the quivering hamper.

When we got to Aunt Ruby's house, we found breakfast laid out on the dining table.

'It isn't much,' said Aunt Ruby. 'But we'll supplement it with what you've brought in the hamper.'

Placing the hamper on the table, she lifted the lid and peered inside. And promptly fainted.

Grandfather picked up the python, took it into the garden, and draped it over a branch of a pomegranate tree.

When Aunt Ruby recovered, she insisted that she had seen a huge snake in the picnic hamper. We showed her the empty basket.

'You're seeing things,' said Grandfather. 'You've been working too hard.'

'Teaching is a very tiring job,' I said solemnly.

Grandmother said nothing. But Popeye broke into loud squawks and whistles, and soon everyone, including a slightly hysterical Aunt Ruby, was doubled up with laughter.

But the snake must have tired of the joke because we never saw it again!

The Kitemaker

There was but one tree in the street known as Gali Ram Nath—an ancient banyan that had grown through the cracks of an abandoned mosque—and little Ali's kite was caught in its branches. The boy, barefoot and clad only in a torn shirt, ran along the cobbled stones of the narrow street to where his grandfather sat nodding dreamily in the sunshine in their back courtyard.

'Grandfather,' shouted the boy. 'My kite has gone!'

The old man woke from his daydream with a start and, raising his head, displayed a beard that would have been white had it not been dyed red with mehendi leaves.

'Did the twine break?' he asked. 'I know that kite twine is not what it used to be.'

'No, Grandfather, the kite is stuck in the banyan tree.'

The old man chuckled. 'You have yet to learn how to fly a kite properly, my child. And I am too old to teach you, that's the pity of it. But you shall have another.'

He had just finished making a new kite from bamboo, paper and thin silk, and it lay in the sun, firming up. It was a pale pink kite, with a small green tail. The old man handed it to Ali, and the boy raised himself on his toes and kissed his grandfather's hollowed-out cheek.

'I will not lose this one,' he said. 'This kite will fly like a bird.' And he turned on his heels and skipped out of the courtyard.

The old man remained dreaming in the sun. His kite shop was gone, the premises long since sold to a junk dealer; but he still made kites, for his own amusement and for the benefit of his grandson, Ali. Not many people bought kites these days. Adults disdained them, and children preferred to spend their money at the cinema. Moreover, there were not many open spaces left for the flying of kites. The city had swallowed up the open grassland that had stretched from the old fort's walls to the river bank.

But the old man remembered a time when grown men flew kites, and great battles were fought, the kites swerving and swooping in the sky, tangling with each other until the string of one was severed. Then the defeated but liberated kite would float away into the blue unknown. There was a good deal of betting, and money frequently changed hands.

Kite flying was then the sport of kings, and the old man remembered how the Nawab himself would come down to the riverside with his retinue to participate in this noble pastime. There was time, then, to spend an idle hour with a gay, dancing strip of paper. Now everyone hurried, in a heat of hope, and delicate things like kites and daydreams were trampled underfoot.

He, Mehmood the kitemaker, had in the prime of his life been well known throughout the city. Some of his more elaborate kites once sold for as much as three or four rupees each.

At the request of the Nawab he had once made a very special kind of kite, unlike any that had been seen in the district. It consisted of a series of small, very light paper disks trailing on a thin bamboo frame. To the end of each disk he fixed a spring of grass, forming a balance on both sides. The surface of the foremost disk was slightly convex, and a fantastic face was painted on it, having two eyes made of small mirrors. The disks, decreasing in size from head to tail, assumed an undulatory form and gave the kite the appearance of a crawling serpent. It required great skill to raise this cumbersome device from the ground, and only Mehmood could manage it.

Everyone had heard of the 'Dragon Kite' that Mehmood had built, and word went round that it possessed supernatural powers. A large crowd assembled in the open to watch its first public launching in the presence of the Nawab.

At the first attempt it refused to leave the ground. The disks made a plaintive, protesting sound, and the sun was trapped in the little mirrors, making the kite a living, complaining creature. Then the wind came from the right direction, and the Dragon Kite soared into the sky, wriggling its way higher and higher, the sun still glinting in its devil eyes. And when it went very high, it pulled fiercely at the twine, and Mehmood's young sons had to help him with the reel. Still the kite pulled, determined to be free, to break loose, to live a life of its own. And eventually it did so.

The twine snapped, the kite leaped away towards the sun, sailing on heavenward until it was lost to view. It was never found again, and Mehmood wondered afterwards if he had made too vivid, too living a thing of the great kite. He did not make another like it. Instead he presented to the Nawab a musical kite, one that made a sound like a violin when it rose into the air.

Those were more leisurely, more spacious days. But the

Nawab had died years ago, and his descendants were almost as poor as Mehmood himself. Kitemakers, like poets, once had their patrons; but now no one knew Mehmood, simply because there were too many people in the Gali, and they could not be bothered with their neighbours.

When Mehmood was younger and had fallen sick, everyone in the neighbourhood had come to ask after his health; but now, when his days were drawing to a close, no one visited him. Most of his old friends were dead and his sons had grown up: one was working in a local garage and the other, who was in Pakistan at the time of the Partition, had not been able to rejoin his relatives.

The children who had bought kites from him ten years ago were now grown men, struggling for a living; they did not have time for the old man and his memories. They had grown up in a swiftly changing and competitive world, and they looked at the old kitemaker and the banyan tree with the same indifference.

Both were taken for granted—permanent fixtures that were of no concern to the raucous, sweating mass of humanity that surrounded them. No longer did people gather under the banyan tree to discuss their problems and their plans; only in the summer months did a few seek shelter from the fierce sun.

But there was the boy, his grandson. It was good that Mehmood's son worked close by, for it gladdened the old man's heart to watch the small boy at play in the winter sunshine, growing under his eyes like a young and well-nourished sapling putting forth new leaves each day. There is a great affinity between trees and men. We grow at much the same pace, if we are not hurt or starved or cut down. In our youth we are resplendent creatures, and in our declining years we stoop a little, we remember, we stretch our brittle limbs in the sun, and then, with a sigh, we shed our last leaves.

Mehmood was like the banyan, his hands gnarled and twisted like the roots of the ancient tree. Ali was like the young mimosa planted at the end of the courtyard. In two years, both he and the tree would acquire the strength and confidence of their early youth.

The voices in the street grew fainter, and Mehmood wondered if he was going to fall asleep and dream, as he so often did, of a kite so beautiful and powerful that it would resemble the great white bird of the Hindus—Garuda, God Vishnu's famous steed. He would like to make a wonderful new kite for little Ali. He had nothing else to leave the boy.

He heard Ali's voice in the distance, but did not realize that the boy was calling him. The voice seemed to come from very far away.

Ali was at the courtyard door, asking if his mother had as yet returned from the bazaar. When Mehmood did not answer, the boy came forward repeating his question. The sunlight was slanting across the old man's head, and a small white butterfly rested on his flowing beard. Mehmood was silent; and when Ali put his small brown hand on the old man's shoulder, he met with no response. The boy heard a faint sound, like the rubbing of marbles in his pocket.

Suddenly afraid, Ali turned and moved to the door, and then ran down the street shouting for his mother. The butterfly left the old man's beard and flew to the mimosa tree, and a sudden gust of wind caught the torn kite and lifted it in the air, carrying it far above the struggling city into the blind blue sky.

Most Beautiful

I don't quite know why I found that particular town so heartless. Perhaps because of its crowded, claustrophobic atmosphere, its congested and insanitary lanes, its weary people... One day I found the children of the bazaar tormenting a deformed, retarded boy.

About a dozen boys, between the ages of eight and fourteen, were jeering at the retard, who was making things worse for himself by confronting the gang and shouting abuses at them. The boy was twelve or thirteen, judging by his face, but had the height of an eight or nine-year-old. His legs were thick, short and bowed. He had a small chest but his arms were long, making him rather ape-like in his attitude. His forehead and cheeks were pitted with the scars of smallpox. He was ugly by normal standards, and the gibberish he spoke did nothing to discourage his tormentors. They threw mud and stones at him, while keeping well out of his reach. Few can be more cruel than a gang of schoolboys in high spirits.

I was an uneasy observer of the scene. I felt that I ought to do something to put a stop to it, but lacked the courage to interfere. It was only when a stone struck the boy on the face, cutting open his cheek, that I lost my normal discretion and ran in amongst the boys, shouting at them and clouting those I could reach. They scattered like defeated soldiery.

I was surprised at my own daring, and rather relieved when the boys did not return. I took the frightened, angry boy by the hand, and asked him where he lived. He drew away from me, but I held on to his fat little fingers and told him I would take him home. He mumbled something incoherent and pointed down a narrow lane. I led him away from the bazaar.

I said very little to the boy because it was obvious that he had some defect of speech. When he stopped outside a door set in a high wall, I presumed that we had come to his house.

The door was opened by a young woman. The boy immediately threw his arms around her and burst into tears. I had not been prepared for the boy's mother. Not only did she look perfectly normal physically, but she was also strikingly handsome. She must have been about thirty-five.

She thanked me for bringing her son home, and asked me into the house. The boy withdrew into a corner of the sitting room, and sat on his haunches in gloomy silence, his bow legs looking even more grotesque in this posture. His mother offered me tea, but I asked for a glass of water. She asked the boy to fetch it, and he did so, thrusting the glass into my hands without looking me in the face.

'Suresh is my only son,' she said. 'My husband is disappointed in him, but I love my son. Do you think he is very ugly?'

'Ugly is just a word,' I said. 'Like beauty. They mean different things to different people. What did the poet say?—"Beauty is truth, truth is beauty." But if beauty and truth are the same thing, why have different words? There are no absolutes except birth and death.'

The boy squatted down at her feet, cradling his head in her lap. With the end of her sari, she began wiping his face.

'Have you tried teaching him to talk properly?' I asked.

'He has been like this since childhood. The doctors can do nothing.'

While we were talking the father came in, and the boy slunk away to the kitchen. The man thanked me curtly for bringing the boy home, and seemed at once to dismiss the whole matter from his mind. He seemed preoccupied with business matters. I got the impression that he had long since resigned himself to having a deformed son, and his early disappointment had changed to indifference. When I got up to leave, his wife accompanied me to the front door.

'Please do not mind if my husband is a little rude,' she said. 'His business is not going too well. If you would like to come again, please do. Suresh does not meet many people who treat him like a normal person.'

I knew that I wanted to visit them again—more out of sympathy for the mother than out of pity for the boy. But I realized that she was not interested in me personally, except as a possible mentor for her son.

After about a week I went to the house again.

Suresh's father was away on a business trip, and I stayed for lunch. The boy's mother made some delicious parathas stuffed with ground radish, and served it with pickle and curd. If Suresh ate like an animal, gobbling his food, I was not far behind him. His mother encouraged him to overeat. He was morose and uncommunicative when he ate, but when I suggested that he come with me for a walk, he looked up eagerly. At the same time a look of fear passed across his mother's face.

'Will it be all right?' she asked. 'You have seen how other children treat him. That day he slipped out of the house without telling anyone.'

'We won't go towards the bazaar,' I said. 'I was thinking of a walk in the fields.'

Suresh made encouraging noises and thumped the table with his fists to show that he wanted to go. Finally his mother consented, and the boy and I set off down the road.

He could not walk very fast because of his awkward legs, but this gave me a chance to point out to him anything that I thought might arouse his interest—parrots squabbling in a banyan tree, buffaloes wallowing in a muddy pond, a group of hermaphrodite musicians strolling down the road. Suresh took a keen interest in the hermaphrodites, perhaps because they were grotesque in their own way: tall, masculine-looking people dressed in women's garments, ankle bells jingling on their heavy feet, and their long, gaunt faces made up with rouge and mascara. For the first time, I heard Suresh laugh. Apparently he had discovered that there were human beings even odder than he was. And like any human being, he lost no time in deriding them.

'Don't laugh,' I said. 'They were born that way, just as you were born the way you are.'

But he did not take me seriously and grinned, his wide mouth revealing surprisingly strong teeth.

We reached the dry riverbed on the outskirts of the town and crossing it entered a field of yellow mustard flowers. The mustard stretched away towards the edge of a subtropical forest. Seeing trees in the distance, Suresh began to run towards them, shouting and clapping his hands. He had never been out of town before. The courtyard of his house and, occasionally, the road to the bazaar, were all that he had seen of the world. Now the trees beckoned him.

We found a small stream running through the forest and I took off my clothes and leapt into the cool water, inviting Suresh to join me. He hesitated about taking off his clothes, but after watching me for a while, his eagerness to join me overcame his self-consciousness, and he exposed his misshapen little body to the soft spring sunshine.

He waded clumsily towards me. The water which came only to my knees reached up to his chest.

'Come, I'll teach you to swim,' I said. And lifting him up from the waist, I held him afloat. He spluttered and thrashed around, but stopped struggling when he found that he could stay afloat.

Later, sitting on the banks of the stream, he discovered a small turtle sitting over a hole in the ground in which it had laid its eggs. He had never watched a turtle before, and watched it in fascination, while it drew its head into its shell and then thrust it out again with extreme circumspection. He must have felt that the turtle resembled him in some respects, with its squat legs, rounded back, and tendency to hide its head from the world.

After that I went to the boy's house about twice a week, and we nearly always visited the stream. Before long Suresh was able to swim a short distance. Knowing how to swim—this was something the bazaar boys never learnt—gave him a certain confidence, made his life something more than a one-dimensional existence.

The more I saw Suresh, the less conscious was I of his deformities. For me, he was fast becoming the norm; while the children of the bazaar seemed abnormal in their very similarity to each other. That he was still conscious of his ugliness—and how could he ever cease to be—was made clear to me about two months after our first meeting.

We were coming home through the mustard fields, which had turned from yellow to green, when I noticed that we were being followed by a small goat. It appeared to have been separated from its mother, and now attached itself to us. Though I tried driving the kid away, it continued tripping along at our heels, and when Suresh found that it persisted in accompanying us, he picked it up and took it home.

The kid became his main obsession during the next few days. He fed it with his own hands and allowed it to sleep at the foot of his bed. It was a pretty little kid, with fairy horns and an engaging habit of doing a hop, skip and jump when moving about the house. Everyone admired the pet, and the boy's mother and I both remarked on how pretty it was.

His resentment against the animal began to show when others started admiring it. He suspected that they found it better-looking than its owner. I remember finding him squatting in front of a low mirror, holding the kid in his arms, and studying their reflections in the glass. After a few minutes of this, Suresh thrust the goat away. When he noticed that I was watching him, he got up and left the room without looking at me.

Two days later, when I called at the house, I found his

mother looking very upset. I could see that she had been crying. But she seemed relieved to see me, and took me into the sitting room. When Suresh saw me, he got up from the floor and ran to the verandah.

'What's wrong?' I asked.

'It was the little goat,' she said. 'Suresh killed it.'

She told me how Suresh, in a sudden and uncontrollable rage, had thrown a brick at the kid, breaking its skull. What had upset her more than the animal's death was the fact that Suresh had shown no regret for what he had done.

'I'll talk to him,' I said, and went out to the verandah, but the boy had disappeared.

'He must have gone to the bazaar,' said his mother anxiously. 'He does that when he's upset. Sometimes I think he likes to be teased and beaten.'

He was not in the bazaar. I found him near the stream, lying flat on his belly in the soft mud, chasing tadpoles with a stick.

'Why did you kill the goat?' I asked.

He shrugged his shoulders.

'Did you enjoy killing it?'

He looked at me and smiled and nodded his head vigorously.

'How very cruel,' I said. But I did not mean it. I knew that his cruelty was no different from mine or anyone else's; only his was an untrammelled cruelty, primitive, as yet undisguised by civilizing restraints.

He took a penknife from his shirt pocket, opened it, and held it out to me by the blade. He pointed to his bare stomach and motioned me to thrust the blade into his belly. He had such a mournful look on his face (the result of having offended me and not in remorse for the goat sacrifice) that I had to burst out laughing.

'You are a funny fellow,' I said, taking the knife from him and throwing it into the stream. 'Come, let's have a swim.'

We swam all afternoon, and Suresh went home smiling. His mother and I conspired to keep the whole affair a secret from his father—who had not in any case been aware of the goat's presence.

Suresh seemed quite contented during the following weeks. And then I received a letter offering me a job in Delhi and I knew that I would have to take it, as I was earning very little from my writing at the time.

The boy's mother was disappointed, even depressed, when I told her I would be going away. I think she had grown quite fond of me. But the boy, always unpredictable, displayed no feeling at all. I felt a little hurt by his apparent indifference. Did our weeks of companionship mean nothing to him? I told myself that he probably did not realize that he might never see me again.

On the evening my train was to leave, I went to the house to say goodbye. The boy's mother made me promise to write to them, but Suresh seemed cold and distant, and refused to sit near me or take my hand. He made me feel that I was an outsider again—one of the mob throwing stones at odd and frightening people.

At eight o'clock that evening I entered a third-class compartment and, after a brief scuffle with several other travellers, succeeded in securing a seat near a window. It enabled me to look down the length of the platform.

The guard had blown his whistle and the train was about to leave when I saw Suresh standing near the station turnstile, looking up and down the platform.

'Suresh!' I shouted and he heard me and came hobbling along the platform. He had run the gauntlet of the bazaar during the busiest hour of the evening.

'I'll be back next year,' I called.

The train had begun moving out of the station, and as I waved to Suresh, he broke into a stumbling run, waving his arms in frantic, restraining gestures.

I saw him stumble against someone's bedding roll and fall sprawling on the ground. The engine picked up speed and the platform receded.

And that was the last I saw of Suresh, lying alone on the crowded platform, alone in the great grey darkness of the world, crooked and bent and twisted—the most beautiful boy in the world.

Voting at Fosterganj

I am standing under the deodars, waiting for a taxi. Devilal, one of the candidates in the civic election, is offering free rides to all his supporters, to ensure that they get to the polls in time. I have assured him that I prefer walking but he does not believe me; he fears that I will settle down with a bottle of beer rather than walk the two miles to the Fosterganj polling station to cast my vote. He has gone to the expense of engaging a taxi for the day just to make certain of lingerers like me. He assures me that he is not using unfair means—most of the other candidates are doing the same thing.

It is a cloudy day, promising rain, so I decide I will wait for the taxi. It has been plying since 6 a.m., and now it is ten o'clock. It will continue plying up and down the hill till 4 p.m. and by that time it will have cost Devilal over a hundred rupees.

Here it comes. The driver—like most of our taxi drivers, a Sikh—sees me standing at the gate, screeches to a sudden stop, and opens the door. I am about to get in when I notice that the windscreen carries a sticker displaying the Congress symbol of the cow and calf. Devilal is an Independent, and has adopted a cock bird as his symbol.

'Is this Devilal's taxi?' I ask.

'No, it's the Congress taxi,' says the driver.

'I'm sorry,' I say. 'I don't know the Congress candidate.'

'That's all right,' he says agreeably; he isn't a local man and has no interest in the outcome of the election. 'Devilal's taxi will be along any minute now.'

He moves off, looking for the Congress voters on whose behalf he has been engaged. I am glad that the candidates have had to adopt different symbols; it has saved me the embarrassment of turning up in a Congress taxi, only to vote for an Independent. But the real reason for using symbols is to help illiterate voters know whom they are voting for when it comes to putting their papers in the ballot box. All through the hill station's mini-election campaign, posters have been displaying candidates' symbols—a car, a radio, a cock bird, a tiger, a lamp—and the narrow, winding roads resound to the cries of children who are paid to shout, 'Vote for the Radio!' or 'Vote for the Cock!'

Presently my taxi arrives. It is already full, having picked up others on the way, and I have to squeeze in at the back with a stout lalain and her bony husband, the local ration-shop owner. Sitting up front, near the driver, is Vinod, a poor, ragged, quite happy-go-lucky youth, who contrives to turn up wherever I happen to be, and frequently involves himself in my activities. He gives me a namaste and a wide grin.

'What are you doing here?' I ask him.

'Same as you, Bond Sahib. Voting. Maybe Devilal will give me a job if he wins.'

'But you already have a job. I thought you were the games-boy at the school.'

'That was last month, Bond Sahib.'

'They kicked you out?'

'They asked me to leave.'

The taxi gathers speed as it moves smoothly down the winding hill road. The driver is in a hurry; the more trips he makes, the more money he collects. We swerve round sharp corners, and every time the lalain's chubby hands, covered with heavy bangles and rings, clutch at me for support. She and her husband are voting for Devilal because they belong to the same caste; Vinod is voting for him in the hope of getting a job; I am voting for him because I like the man. I find him simple, courteous and ready to listen to complaints about drains, street lighting and wrongly assessed taxes. He even tries to do something about these things. He is a tall, cadaverous man, with paan-stained teeth; no Nixon, Heath or Indira Gandhi; but he knows that Fosterganj folk care little for appearances.

Fosterganj is a small ward (one of four in the hill station of Mussoorie); it has about 1,000 voters. An election campaign has, therefore, to be conducted on a person-to-person basis. There is no point in haranguing a crowd at a street corner; it would be a very small crowd. The only way to canvass support is to visit each voter's house and plead one's cause personally. This means making a lot of promises with a perfectly straight face.

The bazaar and village of Fosterganj crouch in a vale on the way down the mountain to Dehra. The houses on either side of the road are nearly all English-looking, most of them built before the turn of the century. The bazaar is Indian, charming and quite prosperous: tailors sit cross-legged before their sewing machines, turning out blazers and tight trousers for the well-to-do students who attend the many public schools that still thrive here; halwais—pot-bellied sweet vendors—spend all day sitting on their haunches in front of giant frying pans; and coolies carry huge loads of timber or cement or grain up the steep hill paths.

The police station, the little Church of the Resurrection, and the ruined brewery were among the earliest buildings in Fosterganj. The brewery is a mound of rubble, but the road that came into existence to serve the needs of the old Crown Brewery is the one that now serves our taxi. Buckle and Co.'s 'Bullock Train' was the chief means of transport in the old days. Mr Bohle, one of the pioneers of brewing in India, started the 'Old Brewery' at Mussoorie in 1830. Two years later he got into trouble with the authorities for supplying beer to soldiers without permission; he had to move elsewhere.

But the great days of the brewery business really began in 1876, when everyone suddenly acclaimed a much-improved brew. The source was traced to Vat 42 in Whymper's Crown Brewery (the one whose ruins we are now passing), and the beer was retasted and retested until the diminishing level of the barrel revealed the perfectly brewed remains of a soldier who had been reported missing some months previously. He had evidently fallen into the vat and been drowned and, unknown to himself, had given the Fosterganj beer trade a real fillip. Apocryphal though this story may sound, I have it on the authority of the owner of the now defunct *Mafasalite Press* who, in a short account of Mussoorie, wrote that 'meat was thereafter recognized as the missing component and was scrupulously added till more modern, and less cannibalistic, means were discovered to satiate the froth-blower.'

Recently, confirmation came from an old Indian hand now living in London. He wrote to me reminiscing of early days in the hill station and had this to say:

> Uncle Georgie Forster was working for the Crown Brewery when a coolie fell in. Coolies were employed to remove scum etc. from the vats. They walked along planks suspended over the vats. Poor devil must have slipped and fallen in. Uncle often told us about the incident and there was no doubt that the beer tasted very good.

What with soldiers and coolies falling into the vats with seeming regularity, one wonders whether there may have been more to these accidents than met the eye. I have a nagging suspicion that Whymper and Buckle may have been the Burke and Hare of Mussoorie's beer industry.

But no beer is made in Mussoorie today, and Devilal probably regrets the passing of the breweries as much as I do. Only the walls of the breweries remain, and these are several feet thick. The roofs and girders must have been removed for use in other buildings. Moss and sorrel grow in the old walls, and wildcats live in dark corners protected from rain and wind.

We have taken the sharpest curves and steepest gradients, and now our taxi moves smoothly along a fairly level road which might pass for a country lane in England were it not for the clumps of bamboo on either side.

A mist has come up the valley to settle over Fosterganj, and out of the mist looms an imposing mansion, Sikander Hall, which is still owned and occupied by the Skinners, descendants of Colonel James Skinner who raised a body of Irregular Horse for the Marathas. This was absorbed by the East India Company's forces in 1803. The cavalry regiment is still known as Skinner's Horse, but of course it is a tank regiment now. Skinner's troops called him 'Sikander' (a corruption of both Skinner and Alexander), and that is the name his property bears. The Skinners who live here now have, quite sensibly, gone in for keeping pigs and poultry.

The next house belongs to the Raja of K but he is unable to maintain it on his diminishing privy purse, and it has been rented out as an ashram for members of a saffron-robed sect who would rather meditate in the hills than in the plains. There was a time when it was only the Sahibs and rajas who could afford to spend the entire 'season' in Mussoorie. The new rich are the industrialists and maharishis. The coolies and rickshaw pullers are no better off than when I was a boy in Mussoorie. They still carry or pull the same heavy loads, for the same pittance, and seldom attain the age of forty. Only their clientele has changed.

One more gate, and here is Colonel Powell in his khaki bush shirt and trousers, a uniform that never varies with the seasons. He is an old shikari; once wrote a book called *The Call of the Tiger*. He is too old for hunting now, but likes to yarn with me when we meet on the road. His wife has gone home to England, but he does not want to leave India.

'It's the mountains,' he was telling me the other day. 'Once the mountains are in your blood, there is no escape. You have to come back again and again. I don't think I'd like to die anywhere else.'

Today there is no time to stop and chat. The taxi driver, with a vigorous blowing of his horn, takes the car round the last bend, and then through the village and narrow bazaar of Fosterganj, stopping about a hundred yards from the polling stations.

There is a festive air about Fosterganj today, I have never seen so many people in the bazaar. Bunting, in the form of rival posters and leaflets, is strung across the street. The tea shops are doing a roaring trade. There is much last-minute canvassing, and I have to run the gamut of various candidates and their agents. For the first time I learn the names of some of the candidates. In all, seven men are competing for this seat.

A schoolboy, smartly dressed and speaking English, is the first to accost me. He says: 'Don't vote for Devilal, sir. He's a big crook. Vote for Jatinder! See, sir, that's his symbol—the bow and arrow.'

'I shall certainly think about the bow and arrow,' I tell him politely.

Another agent, a man, approaches, and says, 'I hope you are going to vote for the Congress candidate.'

'I don't know anything about him,' I say.

'That doesn't matter. It's the party you are voting for. Don't forget it's Mrs Gandhi's party.'

Meanwhile, one of Devilal's lieutenants has been keeping a close watch on both Vinod and me, to make sure that we are not seduced by rival propaganda. I give the man a reassuring smile and stride purposefully towards the polling station, which has been set up in the municipal schoolhouse. Policemen stand at the entrance, to make sure that no one approaches the voters once they have entered the precincts.

I join the patient queue of voters. Everyone is in good humour, and there is no breaking of the line; these are not film stars we have come to see. Vinod is in another line, and grins proudly at me across the passageway. This is the one day in his life on which he has been made to feel really important. And he *is*. In a small constituency like Fosterganj, every vote counts.

Most of my fellow voters are poor people. Local issues mean something to them, affect their daily living. The more affluent can buy their way out of trouble, can pay for small conveniences; few of them bother to come to the polls. But for the 'common man'—the shopkeeper, clerk, teacher, domestic servant, milkman, mule driver—this is a big day. The man he is voting for has promised him something, and the voter means to take the successful candidate up on his promise. Not for another five years will the same fuss be made over the local cobblers, tailors and laundrymen. Their votes are indeed precious.

And now it is my turn to vote. I confirm my name, address and roll number. I am down on the list as 'Rusking Bound', but I let it pass: I might forfeit my right to vote if I raise any objection at this stage! A dab of marking-ink is placed on my forefinger—this is so that I do not come around a second time—and I am given a paper displaying the names and symbols of all the candidates. I am then directed to the privacy of a small booth, where I place the official rubber stamp against Devilal's name. This done, I fold the paper in four and slip it into the ballot box.

All has gone smoothly. Vinod is waiting for me outside. So is Devilal.

'Did you vote for me?' asks Devilal.

It is my eyes that he is looking at, not my lips, when I reply in the affirmative. He is a shrewd man, with many years' experience in seeing through bluff. He is pleased with my reply, beams at me, and directs me to the waiting taxi.

Vinod and I get in together, and soon we are on the road again, being driven swiftly homewards up the winding hill road.

Vinod is looking pleased with himself; rather smug, in fact. 'You did vote for Devilal?' I ask him. 'The symbol of the cock bird?'

He shakes his head, keeping his eyes on the road. 'No, the cow,' he says.

'You ass!' I exclaim. 'Devilal's symbol was the cock, not the cow!'

'I know,' he says, 'but I like the cow better.'*

I subside into silence. It is a good thing no one else in the taxi has been paying any attention to our conversation. It would be a pity to see Vinod turned out of Devilal's taxi and made to walk the remaining mile to the top of the hill. After all, it will be another five years before he gets another free taxi ride.

---

*In spite of Vinod's defection, Devilal won in 1974.

Landour Bazaar

In most North Indian bazaars, there is a clock tower. And like most clocks in clock towers, this one works in fits and starts: listless in summer, sluggish during the monsoon, stopping altogether when it snows in January. Almost every year the tall brick structure gets a coat of paint. It was pink last year. Now it's a livid purple.

From the clock tower at one end to the mule sheds at the other, this old Mussoorie bazaar is a mile long. The tall, shaky three-storey buildings cling to the mountainside, shutting out the sunlight. They are even shakier now that heavy trucks have started rumbling down the narrow street, originally made for nothing heavier than a rickshaw. The street is narrow and damp, retaining all the bazaar smells—sweetmeats frying, smoke from wood or charcoal fires, the sweat and urine of mules, petrol fumes, all these mingle with the smell of mist and old buildings and distant pines.

The bazaar sprang up about 150 years ago to serve the needs of British soldiers who were sent to the Landour convalescent depot to recover from sickness or wounds. The old military hospital, built in 1827, now houses the Defence Institute of

Work Study.** One old resident of the bazaar, a ninety-year-old tailor, can remember the time, in the early years of the century, when the Redcoats marched through the small bazaar on their way to the cantonment church. And they always carried their rifles into church, remembering how many had been surprised in churches during the 1857 uprising.

Today, the Landour bazaar serves the local population, Mussoorie itself being more geared to the needs and interest of tourists. There are a number of silversmiths in Landour. They fashion silver nose-rings, earrings, bracelets and anklets, which are bought by the women from the surrounding Jaunpuri villages. One silversmith had a chest full of old silver rupees. These rupees are sometimes hung on thin silver chains and worn as pendants. I have often seen women in Garhwal wearing pendants or necklaces of rupees embossed with the profiles of Queen Victoria or King Edward VII.

At the other extreme there are the kabari shops, where you can pick up almost everything—a tape recorder discarded by a Woodstock student, or a piece of furniture from grandmother's time in the hill station. Old clothes, Victorian bric-a-brac, and bits of modern gadgetry vie for your attention.

The old clothes are often more reliable than the new. Last winter I bought a new pullover marked 'Made in Nepal' from a Tibetan pavement vendor. I was wearing it on the way home when it began to rain. By the time I reached my cottage, the pullover had shrunk inches and I had some difficulty getting

---

**The Defence Institute of Work Study has been renamed the Institute of Technologic Management.

out of it! It was now just the right size for Bijju, the milkman's twelve-year-old son, and I gave it to the boy. But it continued to shrink at every wash, and it is now being worn by Teju, Bijju's younger brother, who is eight.

At the dark windy corner in the bazaar, one always found an old man hunched up over his charcoal fire, roasting peanuts. He'd been there for as long as I could remember, and he could be seen at almost any hour of the day or night, in all weathers.

He was probably quite tall, but I never saw him standing up. One judged his height from his long, loose limbs. He was very thin, probably tubercular, and the high cheekbones added to the tautness of his tightly stretched skin.

His peanuts were always fresh, crisp and hot. They were popular with small boys, who had a few coins to spend on their way to and from school. On cold winter evenings, there was always a demand for peanuts from people of all ages.

No one seemed to know the old man's name. No one had ever thought of asking. One just took his presence for granted. He was as fixed a landmark as the clock tower or the old cherry tree that grew crookedly from the hillside. He seemed less perishable than the tree, more dependable than the clock. He had no family, but in a way all the world was his family because he was in continuous contact with people. And yet he was a remote sort of being; always polite, even to children, but never familiar. He was seldom alone, but he must have been lonely.

Summer nights he rolled himself up in a thin blanket and slept on the ground beside the dying embers of his fire. During winter he waited until the last cinema show was over, before retiring to the rickshaw coolies' shelter where there was protection from the freezing wind.

Did he enjoy being alive? I often wondered. He was not a joyful person; but then neither was he miserable. Perhaps he was one of those who do not attach overmuch importance to themselves, who are emotionally uninvolved in the life around them, content with their limitations, their dark corners; people on whom cares rest lightly, simply because they do not care at all.

I wanted to get to know the old man better, to sound him out on the immense questions involved in roasting peanuts all one's life; but it's too late now. He died last summer.

That corner remained very empty, very dark, and every time I passed it, I was haunted by visions of the old peanut vendor, troubled by the questions I did not ask; and I wondered if he was really as indifferent to life as he appeared to be.

Then, a few weeks ago, there was a new occupant of the corner, a new seller of peanuts. No relative of the old man, but a boy of thirteen or fourteen. The human personality can impose its own nature on its surroundings. In the old man's time it seemed a dark, gloomy corner. Now it's lit up by sunshine—a sunny personality, smiling, chattering. Old age gives way to youth; and I'm glad I won't be alive when the new peanut vendor grows old. One shouldn't see too many people grow old.

Leaving the main bazaar behind, I walk some way down the Mussoorie–Tehri road, a fine road to walk on, in spite of the dust from an occasional bus or jeep. From Mussoorie to Chamba, a distance of some thirty-five miles, the road seldom descends below 7,000 feet, and there is a continual vista of the snow ranges to the north and valleys and rivers to the south. Dhanaulti is one of the lovelier spots, and the Garhwal Mandal

Vikas Nigam has a rest house here, where one can spend an idyllic weekend. Some years ago I walked all the way to Chamba, spending the night at Kaddukhal, from where a short climb takes one to the Surkhanda Devi temple.

Leaving the Tehri road, one can also trek down to the little Aglar river and then up to Nag Tibba, 9,000 feet, which has good oak forests and animals ranging from barking deer to Himalayan bear; but this is an arduous trek and you must be prepared to spend the night in the open or seek the hospitality of a village.

On this particular day I reach Suakholi and rest in a tea shop, a loose stone structure with a tin roof held down by stones. It serves the bus passengers, mule drivers, milkmen and others who use this road.

I find a couple of mules tethered to a pine tree. The mule drivers, handsome men in tattered clothes, sit on a bench in the shade of the tree, drinking tea from brass tumblers. The shopkeeper, a man of indeterminate age—the cold dry winds from the mountain passes having crinkled his face like a walnut—greets me enthusiastically, as he always does. He even produces a chair, which looks a survivor from one of Wilson's rest houses, and may even be a Sheraton. Fortunately, the Mussoorie kabaris do not know about it or they'd have snapped it up long ago. In any case, the stuffing has come out of the seat. The shopkeeper apologizes for its condition: 'The rats were nesting in it.' And then, to reassure me: 'But they have gone now.'

I would just as soon be on the bench with the Jaunpuri mule drivers, but I do not wish to offend Mela Ram, the tea shop owner; so I take his chair into the shade and lower myself into it.

'How long have you kept this shop?'

'Oh, ten...fifteen years, I do not remember.' He hasn't bothered to count the years. Why should he? Outside the towns in the isolation of the hills, life is simply a matter of yesterday, today and tomorrow. And not always tomorrow.

Unlike Mela Ram, the mule drivers have somewhere to go and something to deliver—sacks of potatoes! From Jaunpur to Jaunsar, the potato is probably the crop best suited to these stony, terraced fields. They have to deliver their potatoes in the Landour bazaar and return to their villages before nightfall; and soon they lead their pack animals away, along the dusty road to Mussoorie.

'Tea or lassi?' Mela Ram offers me a choice, and I choose the curd preparation, which is sharp, sour and very refreshing. The wind soughs gently in the upper branches of the pine trees, and I relax in my Sheraton chair like some eighteenth-century nawab who has brought his own furniture into the wilderness. I can see why Wilson did not want to return to the plains when he came this way in the 1850s. Instead, he went further and higher into the mountains and made his home among the people of the Bhagirathi Valley.

Having wandered some way down the Tehri road, it is quite late by the time I return to the Landour bazaar. Lights still twinkle on the hills, but shop fronts are shuttered and the little bazaar is silent. The people living on either side of the narrow street can hear my footsteps, and I hear their casual remarks, music, a burst of laughter.

Through a gap in the rows of buildings I can see Pari Tibba outlined in the moonlight. A greenish phosphorescent glow appears to move here and there about the hillside. This is the 'fairy light' that gives the hill its name Pari Tibba, Fairy Hill. I have no explanation for it, and I don't know anyone else who has been able to explain it satisfactorily; but often from my window I see this greenish light zigzagging about the hill.

A three-quarter moon is up, and the tin roofs of the bazaar, drenched with dew, glisten in the moonlight. Although the street is unlit, I need no torch. I can see every step of the way. I can even read the headlines on the discarded newspaper lying in the gutter.

Although I am alone on the road, I am aware of the life, pulsating around me. It is a cold night, doors and windows are shut; but through the many clinks, narrow fingers of light reach out into the night. Who could still be up? A shopkeeper going through his accounts, a college student preparing for his exams, someone coughing and groaning in the dark.

Three stray dogs are romping in the middle of the road. It is their road now, and they abandon themselves to a wild chase, almost knocking me down.

A jackal slinks across the road, looking to the right and left—he knows his road-drill—to make sure the dogs have gone. A field rat wriggles through a hole in a rotting plank on its nightly foray among sacks of grain and pulses.

Yes, this is an old bazaar. The bakers, tailors, silversmiths and wholesale merchants are the grandsons of those who followed the mad Sahibs to this hilltop in the 30s and 40s of the last century. Most of them are plainsmen, quite prosperous, even though many of their houses are crooked and shaky.

Although the shopkeepers and tradesmen are fairly

prosperous, the hill people—those who come from the surrounding Tehri and Jaunpur villages—are usually poor. Their small holdings and rocky fields do not provide them with much of a living, and men and boys have to often come into the hill station or go down to the cities in search of a livelihood. They pull rickshaws, or work in hotels and restaurants. Most of them have somewhere to stay.

But as I pass along the deserted street under the shadow of the clock tower, I find a boy huddled in a recess, a thin shawl wrapped around his shoulders. He is wide awake and shivering.

I pass by, my head down, my thoughts already on the warmth of my small cottage only a mile away. And then I stop. It is almost as though the bright moonlight has stopped me, holding my shadow in thrall.

> If I am not for myself,
> Who will be for me?
> And if I am not for others,
> What am I?
> And if not now, when?

The words of an ancient sage beat upon my mind. I walk back to the shadows where the boy crouches. He does not say anything, but he looks up at me, puzzled and apprehensive. All the warnings of well-wishers crowd in upon me—stories of crime by night, of assault and robbery, 'ill met by moonlight'.

But this is not northern Ireland or Lebanon or the streets of New York. This is Landour in the Garhwal Himalayas. And the boy is no criminal. I can tell from his features that he comes from the hills beyond Tehri. He has come here looking for work and has yet to find any.

'Have you somewhere to stay?' I ask.

He shakes his head; but something about my tone of voice has given him confidence, because now there is a glimmer of hope, a friendly appeal in his eyes.

I have committed myself. I cannot pass on. A shelter for the night—that's the very least one human should be able to expect from another.

'If you can walk some way,' I offer, 'I can give you a bed and blanket.'

He gets up immediately, a thin boy, wearing only a shirt and part of an old tracksuit. He follows me without any hesitation. I cannot now betray his trust. Nor can I fail to trust him.

A Night Walk Home

No night is so dark as it seems.

Here in Landour, on the first range of the Himalayas, I have grown accustomed to the night's brightness—moonlight, starlight, lamplight, firelight! Even fireflies light up the darkness.

Over the years, the night has become my friend. On the one hand, it gives me privacy; on the other, it provides me with limitless freedom.

Not many people relish the dark. There are some who will even sleep with their lights burning all night. They feel safer that way. Safer from the phantoms conjured up by their imaginations. A primeval instinct, perhaps, going back to the time when primitive man hunted by day and was in turn hunted by night.

And yet, I have always felt safer by night, provided I do not deliberately wander about on clifftops or roads where danger is known to lurk. It's true that burglars and lawbreakers often work by night, their principal object being to get into other people's houses and make off with the silver or the family jewels. They are not into communing with the stars. Nor are late-night revellers, who are usually to be found in brightly lit places and are thus easily avoided. The odd drunk stumbling home is quite harmless and probably in need of guidance.

I feel safer by night, yes, but then I do have the advantage of living in the mountains, in a region where crime and random violence are comparatively rare. I know that if I were living in a big city in some other part of the world, I would think twice about walking home at midnight, no matter how pleasing the night sky would be.

Walking home at midnight in Landour can be quite eventful, but in a different sort of way. One is conscious all the time of the silent life in the surrounding trees and bushes. I have smelt a leopard without seeing it. I have seen jackals on the prowl. I have watched foxes dance in the moonlight. I have seen flying squirrels flit from one treetop to another. I have observed pine martens on their nocturnal journeys, and listened to the calls of nightjars and owls and other birds who live by night. Not all on the same night, of course. That would be a case of too many riches all at once. Some night walks can be uneventful. But usually there is something to see or hear or sense. Like those foxes dancing in the moonlight. One night, when I got home, I sat down and wrote these lines:

As I walked home last night,
I saw a lone fox dancing
In the bright moonlight.
I stood and watched; then
Took the low road, knowing
The night was his by right.
Sometimes, when words ring true,
I'm like a lone fox dancing
In the morning dew.

Who else, apart from foxes, flying squirrels and night-loving writers are at home in the dark? Well, there are the nightjars, not much to look at, although their large, lustrous eyes gleam uncannily in the light of a lamp. But their sounds are distinctive. The breeding call of the Indian nightjar resembles the sound of a stone skimming over the surface of a frozen pond; it can be heard for a considerable distance. Another species utters a loud grating call which, when close at hand, sounds exactly like a whiplash cutting the air. 'Horsfield's nightjar' (with which I am more familiar in Mussoorie) makes a noise similar to that made by striking a plank with a hammer.

I must not forget the owls, those most celebrated of night birds, much maligned by those who fear the night. Most owls have very pleasant calls. The little jungle owlet has a note which is both mellow and musical. One misguided writer has likened its call to a motorcycle starting up, but this is libel. If only motorcycles sounded like the jungle owl, the world would be a more peaceful place to live and sleep in.

Then there is the little scops owl, who speaks only in monosyllables, occasionally saying 'wow' softly but with great deliberation. He will continue to say 'wow' at intervals of about a minute, for several hours throughout the night.

Probably the most familiar of Indian owls is the spotted owlet, a noisy bird who pours forth a volley of chuckles and squeaks in the early evening and at intervals all night. Towards sunset, I watch the owlets emerge from their holes one after another. Before coming out, each puts out a queer little round head with staring eyes. After they have emerged they usually sit very quietly for a time as though only half awake. Then, all of a sudden, they begin to chuckle, finally breaking out in a torrent of chattering. Having in this way 'psyched' themselves into the right frame of mind, they spread their short, rounded wings and sail off for the night's hunting.

And I wend my way homewards. 'Night with her train of stars' is always enticing. The poet Henley found her so. But he also wrote of 'her great gift of sleep', and it is this gift that I am now about to accept with gratitude and humility.

Foster of Fosterganj

Straddling a spur of the Mussoorie range, as it dips into the Doon valley, Fosterganj came into existence some two hundred years ago and was almost immediately forgotten. And today it is not very different from what it was in 1961, when I lived there briefly.

A quiet corner, where I could live like a recluse and write my stories—that was what I was looking for. And in Fosterganj I thought I'd found my retreat: a cluster of modest cottages, a straggling little bazaar, a post office, a crumbling castle (supposedly haunted), a mountain stream at the bottom of the hill, a winding footpath that took you either uphill or down. What more could one ask for? It reminded me a little of an English village, and indeed that was what it had once been; a tiny settlement on the outskirts of the larger hill station. But the British had long since gone, and the residents were now a fairly mixed lot, as we shall see.

I forget what took me to Fosterganj in the first place. Destiny, perhaps; although I'm not sure why destiny would have bothered to guide an itinerant writer to an obscure hamlet in the hills. Chance would be a better word. For chance plays a great part in all our lives. And it was just by chance that I found myself in the Fosterganj bazaar one fine morning early in May. The oaks and maples were in new leaf; geraniums flourished on sunny balconies; a boy delivering milk whistled a catchy Dev Anand song; a mule train clattered down the street. The chill of winter had gone and there was warmth in the sunshine that played upon old walls.

I sat in a tea shop, tested my teeth on an old bun, and washed it down with milky tea. The bun had been around for some time, but so had I, so we were quits. At the age of forty I could digest almost anything.

The tea shop owner, Melaram, was a friendly sort, as are most tea shop owners. He told me that not many tourists made their way down to Fosterganj. The only attraction was the waterfall, and you had to be fairly fit in order to scramble down the steep and narrow path that led to the ravine where a little stream came tumbling over the rocks. I would visit it one day, I told him.

'Then you should stay here a day or two,' said Melaram. 'Explore the stream. Walk down to Rajpur. You'll need a good walking stick. Look, I have several in my shop. Cherry wood, walnut wood, oak.' He saw me wavering. 'You'll also need one to climb the next hill—it's called Pari Tibba.' I was charmed by the name—Fairy Hill.

I hadn't planned on doing much walking that day—the walk down to Fosterganj from Mussoorie had already taken almost an hour—but I liked the look of a sturdy cherry-wood walking stick, and I bought one for two rupees. Those were the days of simple living. You don't see two-rupee notes any more. You don't see walking sticks either. Hardly anyone walks.

I strolled down the small bazaar, without having to worry about passing cars and lorries or a crush of people. Two or three schoolchildren were sauntering home, burdened by their school bags bursting with homework. A cow and a couple of stray dogs examined the contents of an overflowing dustbin. A policeman sitting on a stool outside a tiny police outpost yawned, stretched, stood up, looked up and down the street in anticipation of crimes to come, scratched himself in the anal region and sank back upon his stool.

A man in a crumpled shirt and threadbare trousers came up to me, looked me over with his watery grey eyes, and said, 'Sir, would you like to buy some gladioli bulbs?' He held up a basket full of bulbs which might have been onions. His chin was covered with a grey stubble, some of his teeth were missing, the remaining ones yellow with neglect.

'No, thanks,' I said. 'I live in a tiny flat in Delhi. No room for flowers.'

'A world without flowers,' he shook his head. 'That's what it's coming to.'

'And where do you plant your bulbs?'

'I grow gladioli, sir, and sell the bulbs to good people like you. My name's Foster. I own the land all the way down to the waterfall.'

For a landowner he did not look very prosperous. But his Foster of Fosterganj name intrigued me. 'Isn't this area called Fosterganj?' I asked.

'That's right. My grandfather was the first to settle here. He was a grandson of Bonnie Prince Charlie who fought the British at Bannockburn. I'm the last Foster of Fosterganj. Are you sure you won't buy my daffodil bulbs?'

'I thought you said they were gladioli.'

'Some gladioli, some daffodils.'

They looked like onions to me, but to make him happy I parted with two rupees (which seemed the going rate in Fosterganj) and relieved him of his basket of bulbs. Foster shuffled off, looking a bit like Chaplin's tramp but not half as dapper. He clearly needed the two rupees. Which made me feel less foolish about spending money that I should have held on to. Writers were poor in those days. Though I didn't feel poor.

Back at the tea shop I asked Melaram if Foster really owned a lot of land.

'He has a broken-down cottage and the right-of-way. He charges people who pass through his property. Spends all the money on booze. No one owns the hillside, it's government land. Reserved forest. But everyone builds on it.'

Just as well, I thought, as I returned to town with my basket of onions. Who wanted another noisy hill station? One Mall Road was more than enough. Back in my hotel room, I was about to throw the bulbs away, but on second thoughts decided to keep them. After all, even an onion makes a handsome plant.

A Magic Oil

A day or two later I was in the bank, run by Vishaal (manager), Negi (cashier), and Suresh (peon). I was sitting opposite Vishaal, who was at his desk, taken up by two handsome paperweights but no papers. Suresh had brought me a cup of tea from the tea shop across the road. There was just one customer in the bank, Hassan, who was making a deposit. A cosy summer morning in Fosterganj: not much happening, but life going on just the same.

In walked Foster. He'd made an attempt at shaving, but appeared to have given up at a crucial stage, because now he looked like a wasted cricketer finally on his way out. The effect was enhanced by the fact that he was wearing flannel trousers that had once been white but were now greenish yellow; the previous monsoon was to blame. He had found an old tie, and this was strung round his neck, or rather his unbuttoned shirt collar. The said shirt had seen many summers and winters in Fosterganj, and was frayed at the cuffs. Even so, Foster looked quite spry, as compared to when I had last seen him.

'Come in, come in!' said Vishaal, always polite to his customers, even those who had no savings. 'How is your gladioli farm?'

'Coming up nicely,' said Foster. 'I'm growing potatoes too.'

'Very nice. But watch out for the porcupines, they love potatoes.'

'Shot one last night. Cut my hands getting the quills out. But porcupine meat is great. I'll send you some the next time I shoot one.'

'Well, keep some ammunition for the leopard. We've got to get it before it kills someone else.'

'It won't be around for two or three weeks. They keep moving, those leopards. He'll circle the mountain, then be back in these parts. But that's not what I came to see you about, Mr Vishaal. I was hoping for a small loan.'

'Small loan, big loan, that's what we are here for. In what way can we help you, sir?'

'I want to start a chicken farm.'

'Most original.'

'There's a great shortage of eggs in Mussoorie. The hotels want eggs, the schools want eggs, the restaurants want eggs. And they have to get them from Rajpur or Dehradun.'

'Hassan has a few hens,' I put in.

'Only enough for home consumption. I'm thinking in terms of hundreds of eggs—and broiler chickens for the table. I want to make Fosterganj the chicken capital of India. It will be like old times, when my ancestor planted the first potatoes here, brought all the way from Scotland!'

'I thought they came from Ireland,' I said. 'Captain Young, up at Landour.'

'Oh well, we brought other things. Like Scotch whisky.'

'Actually, Irish whisky got here first. Captain Kennedy, up in

Simla.' I wasn't Irish, but I was in a combative frame of mind, which is the same as being Irish.

To mollify Foster, I said, 'You did bring the bagpipe.' And when he perked up, I added: 'But the Gurkha is better at playing it.'

This contretemps over, Vishaal got Foster to sign a couple of forms and told him that the loan would be processed in due course and that we'd all celebrate over a bottle of Scotch whisky. Foster left the room with something of a swagger. The prospect of some money coming in—even if it is someone else's—will put any man in an optimistic frame of mind. And for Foster the prospect of losing it was as yet far distant.

I wanted to make a phone call to my bank in Delhi, so that I could have some of my savings sent to me, and Vishaal kindly allowed me to use his phone.

There were only four phones in all of Fosterganj, and there didn't seem to be any necessity for more. The bank had one. So did Dr Bisht. So did Brigadier Bakshi, retired. And there was one in the police station, but it was usually out of order.

The police station, a one-room affair, was manned by a Daroga and a constable. If the Daroga felt like a nap, the constable took charge. And if the constable took the afternoon off, the Daroga would run the place. This worked quite well, as there wasn't much crime in Fosterganj—if you didn't count Foster's illicit still at the bottom of the hill (Scottish hooch, he called the stuff he distilled); or a charming young delinquent called Sunil, who picked pockets for a living (though not in Fosterganj); or the barber who supplemented his income by supplying charas to his agents at some of the boarding schools;

or the man who sold the secretions of certain lizards, said to increase sexual potency—except that it was only linseed oil, used for oiling cricket bats.

I found the last mentioned, a man called Rattan Lal, sitting on a stool outside my door when I returned from the bank.

'*Saande-ka-tel*,' he declared abruptly, holding up a small bottle containing a vitreous yellow fluid. 'Just one application, Sahib, and the size and strength of your valuable member will increase dramatically. It will break down doors, should doors be shut against you. No chains will hold it down. You will be like a stallion, rampant in a field full of fillies. Sahib, you will rule the roost! MemSahibs and beautiful women will fall at your feet.'

'It will get me into trouble, for certain,' I demurred. 'It's great stuff, I'm sure. But wasted here in Fosterganj.'

Rattan Lal would not be deterred. 'Sahib, every time you try it, you will notice an increase in dimensions, guaranteed!'

'Like Pinocchio's nose,' I said in English. He looked puzzled. He understood the word 'nose', but had no idea what I meant.

'Naak?' he said. 'No, Sahib, you don't rub it on your nose. Here, down between the legs,' and he made as if to give a demonstration. I held a hand up to restrain him.

'There was a boy named Pinocchio in a far-off country,' I explained, switching back to Hindi. 'His nose grew longer every time he told a lie.'

'I tell no lies, Sahib. Look, my nose is normal. Rest is very big. You want to see?'

'Another day,' I said.

'Only ten rupees.'

'The bottle or the rest of you?'

'You joke, Sahib,' and he thrust a bottle into my unwilling hands and removed a ten rupee note from my shirt pocket; all done very simply.

'I will come after a month and check up,' he said. 'Next time I will bring the saanda itself! You are in the prime of your life, it will make you a bull among men.' And away he went.

◆

The little bottle of oil stood unopened on the bathroom shelf for weeks. I was too scared to use it. It was like the bottle in Alice in Wonderland with the label DRINK ME. Alice drank it, and shot up to the ceiling. I wasn't sure I wanted to grow that high.

I did wonder what would happen if I applied some of it to my scalp. Would it stimulate hair growth? Would it stimulate my thought processes? Put an end to writer's block?

Well, I never did find out. One afternoon I heard a clatter in the bathroom and looked in to see a large and sheepish looking monkey jump out of the window with the bottle.

But to return to Rattan Lal—some hours after I had been sold the aphrodisiac, I was walking up to town to get a newspaper when I met him on his way down.

'Any luck with the magic oil?' I asked.

'All sold out!' he said, beaming with pleasure. 'Ten bottles sold at the Savoy, and six at Hakman's. What a night it's going to be for them.' And he rubbed his hands at the prospect.

'A very busy night,' I said. 'Either that, or they'll be looking for you to get their money back.'

'I will come next month. If you are still here, I'll keep

another bottle for you. Look there!' He took me by the arm and pointed at a large rock lizard that was sunning itself on the parapet. 'You catch me some of those, and I'll pay you for them. Be my partner. Bring me lizards—not small ones, only big fellows—and I will buy!'

'How do you extract the tel?' I asked.

'Ah, that's a trade secret. But I will show you when you bring me some saandas. Now I must go. My good wife waits for me with impatience.'

And off he went, down the bridle path to Rajpur.

The rock lizard was still on the wall, enjoying its afternoon siesta.

It did occur to me that I might make a living from breeding rock lizards. Perhaps Vishaal would give me a loan. I wasn't making much as a writer.

The Garlands on His Brow

Fame has but a fleeting hold
On the reins in our fast-paced society;
So many of yesterday's heroes crumble.

Shortly after my return from England, I was walking down the main road of my old hometown of Dehra, gazing at the shops and passers-by to see what changes, if any, had taken place during my absence. I had been away three years. Still a boy when I went abroad, I was twenty-one when I returned with some mediocre qualifications to flaunt in the faces of my envious friends. (I did not tell them of the loneliness of those years in exile; it would not have impressed them.) I was nearing the clock tower when I met a beggar coming from the opposite direction. In one respect, Dehra had not changed. The beggars were as numerous as ever, though I must admit they looked healthier.

This beggar had a straggling beard, a hunch, a cavernous chest and unsteady legs on which a number of purple sores were festering. His shoulders looked as though they had once been powerful, and his hands thrusting a begging bowl at me, were still strong.

He did not seem sufficiently decrepit to deserve my charity, and I was turning away when I thought I discerned a gleam of recognition in his eyes. There was something slightly familiar about the man; perhaps he was a beggar who remembered me from earlier years. He was even attempting a smile; showing me a few broken yellow fangs; and to get away from him, I produced a coin, dropped it in his bowl and hurried away.

I had gone about a hundred yards when, with a rush of memory, I knew the identity of the beggar. He was the hero of my childhood, Hassan, the most magnificent wrestler in the entire district.

I turned and retraced my steps, half hoping I wouldn't be able to catch up with the man and he had indeed got lost in the bazaar crowd. Well, I would doubtless be confronted by him again in a day or two Leaving the road, I went into the municipal gardens and stretching myself out on the fresh green February grass, allowed my memory to journey back to the days when I was a boy of ten, full of health and optimism, when my wonder at the great game of living had yet to give way to disillusionment at its shabbiness.

On those precious days when I played truant from school—and I would have learnt more had I played truant more often—I would sometimes make my way to the akhara at the corner of the gardens to watch the wrestling pit. My chin cupped in my hands, I would lean against a railing and gaze in awe at the rippling muscles, applauding with the other watchers whenever one of the wrestlers made a particularly clever move or pinned an opponent down on his back.

Amongst these wrestlers the most impressive and engaging

young man was Hassan, the son of a kitemaker. He had a magnificent build, with great wide shoulders and powerful legs, and what he lacked in skill he made up for in sheer animal strength and vigour. The idol of all small boys, he was followed about by large numbers of us, and I was a particular favourite of his. He would offer to lift me on to his shoulders and carry me across the akhara to introduce me to his friends and fellow wrestlers.

From being Dehra's champion, Hassan soon became the outstanding representative of his art in the entire district. His technique improved, he began using his brain in addition to his brawn, and it was said by everyone that he had the makings of a national champion.

It was during a large fair towards the end of the rains that destiny took a hand in the shaping of his life. The Rani of—was visiting the fair, and she stopped to watch the wrestling bouts. When she saw Hassan stripped and in the ring, she began to take more than a casual interest in him. It has been said that she was a woman of a passionate and amoral nature, who could not be satisfied by her weak and ailing husband. She was struck by Hassan's perfect manhood, and through an official offered him the post of her personal bodyguard.

The Rani was rich and, in spite of having passed her fortieth summer, was a warm and attractive woman. Hassan did not find it difficult to make love according to the bidding, and on the whole he was happy in her service. True, he did not wrestle as often as in the past; but when he did enter a competition, his reputation and his physique combined to overawe his opponents, and they did not put up much resistance. One or two well-known wrestlers were invited to the district. The Rani paid them liberally, and they permitted Hassan to throw them out of the ring. Life in the Rani's house was comfortable and easy, and Hassan, a simple man, felt himself secure. And it is to the credit of the Rani (and also of Hassan) that she did not tire of him as quickly as she had of others.

But ranis, like washerwomen, are mortal; and when a long-standing and neglected disease at last took its toll, robbing her at once of all her beauty, she no longer struggled against it, but allowed it to poison and consume her once magnificent body. It would be wrong to say that Hassan was heartbroken when she died. He was not a deeply emotional or sensitive person. Though he could attract the sympathy of others, he had difficulty in producing any of his own. His was of kind but not compassionate nature.

He had served the Rani well, and what he was most aware of now was that he was without a job and without any money. The Raja had his own personal amusements and did not want a wrestler who was beginning to sag a little about the waist.

Times had changed. Hassan's father was dead, and there was no longer a living to be had from making kites; so Hassan returned to doing what he had always done: wrestling. But there was no money to be made at the akhara. It was only in the professional arena that a decent living could be made. And so, when a travelling circus of professionals—a Negro, a Russian, a Cockney-Chinese and a giant Sikh—came to town and offered a hundred rupees and a contract to the challenger who could stay five minutes in the ring with any one of them, Hassan took up the challenge.

He was pitted against the Russian, a bear of a man, who wore a black mask across his eyes; and in two minutes Hassan's Dehra supporters saw their hero slung about the ring, licked in the head and groin, and finally flung unceremoniously through the ropes.

After this humiliation, Hassan did not venture into competitive bouts again. I saw him sometimes at the akhara, where he made a few rupees giving lessons to children. He had a paunch, and folds were beginning to accumulate beneath his chin. I was no longer a small boy, but he always had a smile and a hearty backslap reserved for me.

I remember seeing him a few days before I went abroad. He was moving heavily about the akhara; he had lost the lightning swiftness that had once made him invincible. Yes, I told myself.

The garlands wither on your brow;
They boast no more your mighty deeds...

That had been over three years ago. And for Hassan to have been reduced to begging was indeed a sad reflection of both the passing of time and the changing times. Fifty years ago, a popular local wrestler would never have been allowed to fall into a state of poverty and neglect. He would have been fed by his old friends, and stories would have been told of his legendary prowess. He would not have been forgotten. But those were more leisurely times, when the individual had his place in society, when a man was praised for his past achievement, and his failures were tolerated and forgiven. But life had since become fast and cruel and unreflective, and people were too busy counting their gains to bother about the idols of their youth.

It was a few days after my last encounter with Hassan that I found a small crowd gathered at the side of the road, not far from the clock tower. They were staring impassively at something in the drain, at the same time keeping a discreet distance. Joining the group, I saw that the object of their disinterested curiosity was a corpse, its head hidden under a culvert, legs protruding into the open drain. It looked as though the man had crawled into the drain to die, and had done so with his head in the culvert so the world would not witness his last unavailing struggle.

When the municipal workers came in their van, and lifted the body out of the gutter, a cloud of flies and bluebottles rose from the corpse with an angry buzz of protest. The face was muddy, but I recognized the beggar who was Hassan.

In a way, it was a consolation to know that he had been forgotten, that no one present could recognize the remains of the man who had once looked like a young god. I did not come forward to identify the body. Perhaps I saved Hassan from one final humiliation.

A Guardian Angel

I can still picture the little Dilaram Bazaar as I first saw it twenty years ago. Hanging on the hem of Aunt Mariam's sari, I had followed her along the sunlit length of the dusty road and up the wooden staircase to her rooms above the barber's shop.

There were a number of children playing on the road and they all stared at me. They must have wondered what my dark, black-haired aunt was doing with a strange child who was fairer than most. She did not bother to explain my presence and it was several weeks before the bazaar people learned something of my origins.

Aunt Mariam, my mother's younger sister, was at that time about thirty. She came from a family of Christian converts, originally Muslims of Rampur. My mother had married an Englishman who died while I was still a baby. She herself was not a strong woman and fought a losing battle with tuberculosis while bringing me up.

My sixth birthday was approaching when she died, in the middle of the night, without my being aware of it. And I woke up to experience, for a day, all the terrors of abandonment.

But that same evening Aunt Mariam arrived. Her warmth, worldliness and carefree chatter gave me the reassurance I needed so badly. She slept beside me that night and the next morning, after the funeral, took me with her to her rooms in the bazaar. This small flat was to be my home for the next year and a half.

Before my mother's death I had seen very little of my aunt. From the remarks I occasionally overheard, it appeared that Aunt Mariam had, in some indefinable way, disgraced the family. My mother was cold towards her and I could not help wondering why, because a more friendly and cheerful extrovert than Aunt Mariam could hardly be encountered.

There were other relatives, but they did not come to my rescue with the same readiness. It was only later, when the financial issues became clearer, that innumerable uncles and aunts appeared on the scene.

The age of six is the beginning of an interesting period in the life of a boy, and the months I spent with Aunt Mariam are not difficult to recall. She was a joyous, bubbling creature—a force of nature rather than a woman—and every time I think of her, I am tempted to put down on paper some aspect of her conversation, or her gestures, or her magnificent physique.

She was a strong woman, taller than most men in the bazaar, but this did not detract from her charms. Her voice was warm and deep, her face was a happy one, broad and unlined, and her teeth gleamed white in the dark brilliance of her complexion.

She had large, soft breasts, long arms and broad thighs. She was majestic and at the same time graceful. Above all, she was warm and full of understanding, and it was this tenderness of hers that overcame resentment and jealousy in other women.

She called me ladla, her darling, and told me she had always wanted to look after me. She had never married. I did not, at that age, ponder on the reasons for her single status. At six I took all things for granted, and accepted Mariam for what she was—my benefactress and guardian angel.

Her rooms were untidy compared with the neatness of my mother's house. Mariam revelled in untidiness. I soon grew accustomed to the topsy-turviness of her rooms and found them comfortable. Beds (hers a very large and soft one) were usually left unmade, while clothes lay draped over chairs and tables.

A large watercolour hung on a wall, but Mariam's bodice and knickers were usually suspended from it, and I cannot recall the subject of the painting. The dressing table was a fascinating place, crowded with all kinds of lotions, mascaras, paints, oils and ointments.

Mariam would spend much time sitting in front of the mirror running a comb through her long black hair or preferably having young Mulia, a servant girl, comb it for her. Though a Christian, my aunt retained several Muslim superstitions, and never went into the open with her hair falling loose.

Once, Mulia came into the rooms with her own hair open. 'You ought not to leave your hair open. Better knot it,' said Aunt Mariam.

'But I have not yet oiled it, Aunty,' replied Mulia. 'How can I put it up?'

'You are too young to understand. There are Jinns—aerial spirits—who are easily attracted by long hair and pretty, black eyes like yours.'

'Do Jinns visit human beings, Aunty?'

'Learned people say so. Though I have never seen a Jinn

myself, I have seen the effect they can have on one.'

'Oh, do tell me about them,' said Mulia.

'Well, there was once a lovely girl like you who had a wealth of black hair,' said Mariam. 'Quite unaccountably she fell ill, and in spite of every attention and the best medicines she kept getting worse. She grew as thin as a whipping post, her beauty decayed, and all that remained of it till her dying day was her wonderful head of hair.'

It did not take me long to make friends in Dilaram Bazaar. At first I was an object of curiosity, and when I came down to play in the street, both women and children would examine me as though I was a strange marine creature.

'How fair he is,' observed Mulia.

'And how black his aunt,' commented the washerman's wife, whose face was riddled with the marks of smallpox. 'His skin is very smooth,' pointed out Mulia, who took considerable pride in having been the first to see me at close quarters. She pinched my cheeks with obvious pleasure. 'His hair and eyes are black,' remarked Mulia's ageing mother. 'Is it true that his father was an Englishman?'

'Mariam-bi says so,' said Mulia. 'She never lies.'

'True,' said the washerman's wife. 'Whatever her faults—and there are many—she has never been known to lie.'

My aunt's other 'faults' were a deep mystery to me. Nor did anyone try to enlighten me about them.

Some nights she had me sleep with her, other nights (I often wondered why) she gave me a bed in an adjoining room, although I much preferred remaining with her—especially since, on cold January nights, she provided me with considerable warmth.

I would curl up into a ball just below her soft tummy. On the other side, behind her knees, slept Leila, an enchanting Siamese cat given to her by an American businessman, whose house she would sometimes visit. Every night, before I fell asleep, Mariam would kiss me, very softly, on my closed eyelids. I never fell asleep until I had received this phantom kiss.

At first, I resented the nocturnal visitors that Aunt Mariam frequently received. Their arrival meant that I had to sleep in the spare room with Leila. But when I found that these people were impermanent creatures, mere ships that passed in the night, I learned to put up with them.

I seldom saw those men, though occasionally I caught a glimpse of a beard or an expensive waistcoat or white pyjamas. They did not interest me very much, though I did have a vague idea that they provided Aunt Mariam with some sort of income, thus enabling her to look after me.

Once, when one particular visitor was very drunk, Mariam had to force him out of the flat. I glimpsed this episode through a crack in the door. The man was big but no match for Aunt Mariam.

She thrust him out on to the landing, and then he lost his footing and went tumbling downstairs. No damage was done and the man called on Mariam again a few days later, very sober and contrite, and was readmitted to my aunt's favours.

Aunt Mariam must have begun to worry about the effect these comings and goings might have on me, because after a few months, she began to make arrangements for sending me to a boarding school in the hills.

I had not the slightest desire to go to school, and raised many objections. We had long arguments in which she tried vainly to impress upon me the desirability of receiving an education.

'To make a living, my Ladla,' she said, 'you must have an education.'

'But you have no education,' I said, 'and you have no difficulty in making a living!'

Mariam threw up her arms in mock despair. 'Ten years from now, I will not be able to make such a living. Then who will support and help me? An illiterate young fellow or an educated gentleman? When I am old, my son, when I am old.'

Finally, I succumbed to her arguments and agreed to go to a boarding school. And when the time came for me to leave, both Aunt Mariam and I broke down and wept at the railway station.

I hung out of the window as the train moved away from the platform, and saw Mariam, her bosom heaving, being helped from the platform by Mulia and some of our neighbours.

My incarceration in a boarding school was made more unbearable by the absence of any letters from Aunt Mariam. She could write little more than her name.

I was looking forward to my winter holidays and my return to Aunt Mariam and Dilaram Bazaar, but this was not to be. During my absence, there had been some litigation over my custody, and my father's relatives claimed that Aunt Mariam was not a fit person to be a child's guardian.

And so when I left school, it was not to Aunt Mariam's place that I was sent, but to a strange family living in a railway colony near Moradabad. I remained with these relatives until I finished school. But that is a different story.

I did not see Aunt Mariam again. Dilaram Bazaar and

my beautiful aunt and the Siamese cat all became part of the receding world of my childhood.

I would often think of Mariam, but as time passed, she became more remote and inaccessible in my memory. It was not until many years later, when I was a young man, that I visited Dilaram Bazaar again. I knew from my foster parents that Aunt Mariam was dead. Her heart, it seemed, had always been weak.

I was anxious to see Dilaram Bazaar and its residents again, but my visit was a disappointment. The place had disappeared. Or rather, it had been swallowed up by a growing city. It was lost in the complex of a much larger market, which had sprung up to serve a new govermnent colony. The older people had died, and the young ones had gone to colleges or factories or offices in different towns. Aunt Marianm's rooms had been pulled down.

I found her grave in the little cemetery on the town's outskirts. One of her more devoted admirers had provided a handsome gravestone surmounted by a sculptured angel. One of the wings had broken off and the face was chipped, which gave the angel a slightly crooked smile.

But in spite of the broken wing and the smile, it was a very ordinary stone angel and could not hold a candle to my Aunt Mariam, the very special guardian angel of my childhood.

The Zigzag Walk

Uncle Ken always maintained that the best way to succeed in life was to zigzag. 'If you keep going off in new directions,' he declared, 'you will meet new career opportunities!'

Well, opportunities certainly came Uncle Ken's way, but he was not a success in the sense that Dale Carnegie or Deepak Chopra would have defined a successful man...

In a long life devoted to 'muddling through' with the help of the family, Uncle Ken's many projects had included a chicken farm (rather like the one operated by Ukridge in Wodehouse's *Love Among the Chickens*) and a mineral water bottling project. For this latter enterprise, he bought a thousand old soda-water bottles and filled them with sulphur water from the springs, five miles from Dehra. It was good stuff, taken in small quantities, but drunk one bottle at a time it proved corrosive—'sulphur and brimstone' as one irate customer described it—and angry buyers demonstrated in front of the house, throwing empty bottles over the wall into grandmother's garden.

Grandmother was furious—more with Uncle Ken than with the demonstrators—and made him give everyone's money back.

'You have to be healthy and strong to take sulphur water,'

he explained later.

'I thought it was supposed to make you healthy and strong,' I said.

Grandfather remarked that it did not compare with plain soda-water, which he took with his whisky. 'Why don't you just bottle soda-water?' he said, 'there's a much bigger demand for it.'

But Uncle Ken believed that he had to be original in all things.

'The secret to success is to zigzag,' he said.

'You certainly zigzagged round the garden when your customers were throwing their bottles back at you,' said Grandmother.

Uncle Ken also invented the zigzag walk.

The only way you could really come to know a place well, was to walk in a truly haphazard way. To make a zigzag walk you take the first turning to the left, the first to the right, then the first to the left and so on. It can be quite fascinating provided you are in no hurry to reach your destination. The trouble was that Uncle Ken used this zigzag method even when he had a train to catch.

When Grandmother asked him to go to the station to meet Aunt Mabel and her children, who were arriving from Lucknow, he zigzagged through the town, taking in the botanical gardens in the west and the limestone factories to the east, finally reaching the station by way of the goods yard, in order as he said, 'to take them by surprise'.

Nobody was surprised, least of all Aunt Mabel who had taken a tonga and reached the house while Uncle Ken was still sitting on the station platform, waiting for the next train to come in. I was sent to fetch him.

'Let's zigzag home again,' he said.

'Only on one condition, we eat chaat every fifteen minutes,' I said.

So we went home by way of all the most winding bazaars, and in North Indian towns they do tend to zigzag, stopping at numerous chaat and halwai shops, until Uncle Ken had finished his money. We got home very late and were scolded by everyone; but as Uncle Ken told me, we were pioneers and had to expect to be misunderstood and even maligned. Posterity would recognize the true value of zigzagging.

'The zigzag way,' he said, 'is the diagonal between heart and reason.'

In our more troubled times, had he taken to preaching on the subject, he might have acquired a large following of dropouts. But Uncle Ken was the original dropout. He would not have tolerated others.

Had he been a space traveller, he would have gone from star to star, zigzagging across the Milky Way.

Uncle Ken would not have succeeded in getting anywhere very fast, but I think he did succeed in getting at least one convert (myself) to see his point: 'When you zigzag, you are not choosing what to see in this world but you are giving the world a chance to see you!'

The India I Carried with Me

Am now going back in time, to a period when I was caught between East and West, and had to make up my mind just where I belonged. I had been away from India for barely a month before I was longing to return. The insularity of the place where I found myself (Jersey, in the Channel Islands) had something to do with it, I suppose. There was little there to remind me of India or the East, not one brown face to be seen in the streets or on the beaches. I'm sure it's a different sort of place now; but fifty years ago it had nothing to offer by way of companionship or good cheer to a lonely, sensitive boy who had left home and friends in search of a 'better future'.

I had come to England with a dream of sorts, and I was to return to India with another kind of dream; but in between (there were to be four years of dreary office work, lonely bed-sitting rooms, shabby lodging houses, cheap snack bars, hospital wards, and the struggle to write my first book and find a publisher for it.

I started work in a large departmental store called *Le Riche*. At eight in the morning, when I walked to the store, it was dark. At six in the evening, when I walked home, it was dark again. Where were all those sunny beaches Jersey was famous for? I would have to wait for summer to see them, and a Saturday afternoon to take a dip in the sea.

Occasionally, after an early supper, I would walk along the deserted seafront. If the tide was in and the wind approaching gale-force, the waves would climb the sea wall and drench me with their cold salt spray. My aunt, with whom I was staying, thought I was quite mad to take this solitary walk; but I have always been at one with nature, even in its wilder moments, and the wind and the crashing waves gave me a sense of freedom, strengthened my determination to escape from the island and go my own way.

When I wasn't walking along the seafront, I would sit at the portable typewriter in my small attic room, and hammer out the rough chapters of the book that was to become my first novel. These were characters and incidents based on the journal I had kept during my last year in India. It was 1951, recalled in late 1952. An eighteen-year-old looking back on incidents in the life of a seventeen-year-old! Nostalgia and longing suffused those pages. How I longed to be back with my friends in the small town of Dehra Dun—a leafy place, sunny, fruit-laden, easy-going every familiar corner etched clearly in my memory. Somehow, it had been that last year in Dehra that had brought me closer to the India that I had so far only taken for granted. An India of close and sometimes sentimental friendships. Of striking contrasts: a small cinema showing English pictures (a George Formby comedy or an American musical) and only a couple of hours away thousands taking a dip in the sacred water of the Ganga. Or outside the station, hundreds of pony-drawn tongas waiting to pick up passengers, while the more affluent climbed into their Ford Convertibles, Morris Minors, Baby Austins or flashy Packards and Daimlers.

But of course Dehra in the 'fifties' was a town of bicycles. Students, shopkeepers, Army cadets, office workers, all used them. The scooter (or Lanlbretta) had only just been invented, and it would be several years before it took over from the bicycle. It was still unaffordable for the great majority.

I was awkward on a bicycle and frequently fell off, breaking my arm on one occasion. But this did not prevent me from joining my friends on cycle rides to the Sulphur springs, or to Premnagar (where the Military Academy was situated) or along the Haridwar road and down to the riverbed at Lachiwala.

In Jersey, I found an old cycle belonging to my cousin, and I rode from St. Helier where we lived, to St. Brelade's Bay, at the other end of the island. But returning after dark, I was hauled up for riding without lights. I had no idea that cycles had also to be equipped with lights. Back in Dehra, we never used them!

The attic room had no view, so one of my favourite occupations, gazing out of windows, came to a stop. But perhaps this was helpful in that it made me concentrate on the sheet of paper in my typewriter. After about six months, I had a book of sorts ready for submission to any publisher who was prepared to look at it. Meanwhile, I had been through at least three jobs and had even been offered a post in the Jersey Civil Service, having successfully taken the local civil service exam—something I had done out of sheer boredom, as I had no intention of settling permanently on the island.

I had been keeping a diary of sorts and in some of the entries I had expressed my desire to get back to India, and my discontent at having to stay with relatives who were unsympathetic, not only to my feelings for India but also to my ambitions to become a writer. The diary fell into my uncle's hands. He read it, and was naturally upset. We had a row. I was contrite; but a few days later I packed my suitcases (all two of them) and stepped on to the ferry that was to take me to Southampton and then to London. Lesson one: don't leave your personal diaries lying around!

But perhaps it was all for the best, otherwise I might have hung around in Jersey for another year or two, to the detriment of my personal happiness and my writing ambitions.

I arrived in London in the middle of a thick yellow November fog—those were the days of the killer London fogs—and after a search found the Students' Hostel where I was given a cubicle to myself. But I did not stay there very long; the available food was awful. As soon as I got an office job—not too difficult in the 1950s—I rented an attic room in Belsize Park, the first of many bed-sitters that I was to live in during my three-year sojourn in London.

From Belsize Park I was to move to Haverstock Hill (close to Hampstead Heath), then to South London for a short time, and finally to Swiss Cottage. Most of my landladies were Jewish—refugees from persecution in pre-war Europe—and I too was a refugee of sorts, still very unsure of where I belonged. Was it England, the land of my father, or India, the land of my birth? But my father had also been born in India, had grown up and made a living there, visiting *his* father's land, England, only a couple of times during his life.

The link with Britain was tenuous, based on heredity rather

than upbringing. It was more in the mind. It was a literary England I had been drawn to, not a physical England. And in fact, I took several exploratory walks around 'literary' London, visiting houses or streets where famous writers had once lived; in particular the East End and Dockland, for I had grown up on the novels and stories of Dickens, Smollett, Captain Marryat, and W.W. Jacobs. But I did not make many English friends. If they were a reserved race, I was even more reserved. Always shy, I waited for others to take the initiative. In India, people will take the initiative, they lose no time in getting to know you. Not so in England. They were too polite to look at you. And in that respect, I was more English than the English.

The gentleman who lived on the floor below me occasionally went so far as to greet me with the observation, 'Beastly weather, isn't it?'

And I would respond by saying, 'Oh, perfectly beastly,' and pass on.

How different it was when I bumped into a Gujarati boy, Praveen, who lived on the basement floor. He gave me a winning smile, and I remember saying, 'Oh, to be in Bombay now that winter's here,' and immediately we were friends.

He was only seventeen, a year or two younger than me, and he was studying at one of the polytechnics with a view to getting into the London School of Economics. At that time, most of the Indians in London were students, the great immigration rush was still a long way off,, and racial antagonisms were directed more at the recently arrived West Indians than at Asians.

Praveen took me on the rounds of the coffee bars, then proliferating all over London, and introduced me to other students, among them a Vietnamese, called Thanh, who cultivated my friendship because, as he said, 'I want to speak English.' When he discovered that my accent was very un-English (you could have called it Welsh with an Anglo-Indian interaction), he dropped me like a hot brick. He was very frank, he was not interested in friendship, he said, only in improving his accent. I heard later that he'd attached himself to a young journalist from up north, who spoke broad Yorkshire.

Most evenings I remained in my room and worked on my novel. From being a journal it had become a first person narrative, and now I was turning it into fiction in the third person. The title had also undergone a few changes, but finally I settled on *The Room on the Roof.*

Into it, I put all the love and affection I felt for the friends I had left behind in Dehra. It was more than nostalgia, it was a recreation of the people, places and incidents of that last year in India. I did not want it to fade away. The riverbanks at Haridwar, the mango-groves of the Doon, the poinsettias and bougainvillaea, the games on the parade ground, the chaat shops near the Clock Tower, the summer heat, the monsoon downpours, romping naked in the rain, sitting on railway platforms, gnawing at a stick of sugar cane, listening to street cries... All this and more came crowding upon me as I sat writing before the gas fire in my little room.

When it grew very cold, I used an old overcoat given to me by Diana Athill, the junior partner at Andre Deutsch, who had promised to publish *The Room* if I rewrote it as a novel. Another who encouraged me was a BBC producer, Prudence Smith, who got me to give a couple of talks on Radio's Third

Programme. I felt I was getting somewhere; and when I found myself confined to the Hampstead General Hospital for almost a month, with a mysterious disease which had affected the vision in my right eye, I used the left to catch up on my reading and to write a couple of short stories.

A nurse brought a tray of books around the ward every afternoon, and thanks to this courtesy, I was able to discover the delightful stories of William Saroyan and Denton Welch's sensitive first novel *Maiden Voyage*. Saroyan, a Pulitzer Prize winner for his play *The Time of Your Life*, was then very successful and popular. Denton's promising career had been cut short by a terrible accident. Out cycling on a country road, he had been knocked down by a speeding motorist. He had lived for several years, struggling against crippling injuries and almost completing his sensitive autobiography *A Voice in the Clouds*. He was thirty-one when he died. Towards the end, he could only work for three or four minutes at a time. Complications set in, and the left side of his heart started failing. Even then he made a terrific effort to finish his book. His friend Eric wrote—'Denton was upheld by the high courage which seemed somehow the fruit of his rare intelligence.'

The work of these writers, together with the bottle of Guinness I was given every day as a tonic (they had found me somewhat undernourished), meant that I walked out of the hospital with a spring in my step and a determination to succeed.

But Andre Deutsch was still dithering over my book. The firm was doing well, but he didn't like taking risks. No publisher likes losing money. And he wasn't going to make much out of my novel, a subjective and unsensational work.

But I resented his indecision. So I returned the small amount he'd paid me by way of an option, and demanded the return of my manuscript. Back came an apologetic letter and an advance (then £50) against publication.

Today, almost fifty years later, the firm of Andre Deutsch has gone, but *The Room on the Roof* is still in print, still making friends. This is not something that I gloat over, it only goes to show that books are unpredictable commodities, and that the most successful authors and publishers often fall by the wayside. Publishers go out of business, writers fade from the public mind. Even Saroyan is forgotten now. I'll be forgotten too, someday.

There were to be further delays before The *Room* was published, and I was back in India when it did come out. By then I'd almost forgotten about the book! But it picked up the John Llewellyn Rhys Prize, an award that also went to V.S. Naipaul a year later, for his first book. It was then worth only £50. There were no big sponsors in those days. It is now sponsored by a British newspaper and is worth £5,000. This was turned down last year by another Indian writer, who disagreed with the paper's policies.

Meanwhile, in London, there were other distractions. I loved stage musicals, and if I had a little money to spare I went to the theatre, taking in such productions as *Porgy and Bess, Paint Your Wagon, Pal Joey, Teahouse of the August Moon,* and the occasional review. And of course the annual presentation of *Peter Pan* at the Scala theatre, not far from where I worked. I had grown up on Peter Pan, first read to me by my father in distant Jamnagar, and at school I had read Barrie's other plays and been charmed by them; but, like operetta, they had gone out of fashion and only the ageless Peter remained. 'Do you believe in fairies?' he asks in the play. And to save Tinker Bell from extinction, I clapped with the rest of the audience. But did I really believe in fairies? I looked for them in Kensington Gardens, where Peter Pan's statue stood, and found a few mothers pushing their perambulators, but no fairies. And I looked in Hyde Park, but found only courting couples. And I looked all over Leicester Square, but instead of fairies I found prostitutes soliciting business. As I was still looking for romance, I crept back to my room and my portable typewriter—I would have to create my own romance.

The small portable had been in the windows of a Jersey department store, and every time I passed the store I glanced at the window to see if the typewriter was still there. It seemed to be waiting for me to come in and take it away. I longed to buy it, partly because I had to type out the final drafts of my book, and also because it looked very dainty and attractive. It was definitely out to seduce me. Finally, with the help of a loan from Mr Bromley, a kindly senior clerk, I bought the machine. It cost only £12, but that was three month's wages at the time. It accompanied me to London, and then a couple of years later to India, giving me good service in Dehra Dun, New Delhi, and then Mussoorie where it finally succumbed to the damp monsoon climate.

My worldly possessions had increased, not only by the typewriter, but also by a record player which I had bought second-hand from a Thai student. I had become an ardent fan of the black singer, Eartha Kitt, and had bought all her records;

but they were no good without a player until the Thai boy came to my rescue. Then the sensual, throaty voice of Eartha reverberated through the lodging house, bringing complaints from the landlady and the gentleman downstairs. I had to keep the volume low, which wasn't much fun.

I was also fond of the clarinet (turj) playing of an Indian musician, Master Ibrahim, and I had some of his recordings which transported me back to the streets and bazaars of small-town India. Light, lilting and tuneful, I preferred this sort of flute music to the warblings of the more popular songsters.

Praveen liked gangster films and wanted me to accompany him to anything which featured Humphrey Bogart, James Cagney, George Raft and other tough guys. Praveen wanted to be a tough guy himself and often struck a Bogart-like pose, cigarette dangling from the side of his mouth. There was nothing tough about Praveen, who was really rather delicate, but his affectations were charming and risible.

One day he announced that he was returning to India for a few months, as his ailing mother was anxious to see him. He asked me to come along too, to give him company during the three week voyage. To do so, I would have to throw up my job, but I had already thrown up several jobs. They were simply stop-gaps until I could establish myself as a writer. I hadn't the slightest intention or ambition of being a senior clerk or even an executive for the firm in which I was working. The only problem in leaving England then was that I would have to leave my book in limbo, as there was still no guarantee that Deutsch would publish it. But it was time I went on to write other things; time to strike out on my own, to take a chance with

India. The ships were full of British and Anglo-Indian families coming to England, to make a 'better future' for themselves. I would do the opposite, go into reverse, and make my future, for good or ill, in the land of my birth.

My passport was in order, and I had only to give a week's notice to my employers. I had saved up about £200, and of this £50 went on the cost of my passage, London to Bombay. Praveen and I boarded the S.S. *Balory*, a Polish liner with a reputation for running into trouble. We had no difficulty in securing berths in tourist class. Praveen had every intention of returning to England to complete his studies. My own intentions were very vague. I knew there would be no job for me in India, but I was quietly confident that I could make a living from writing, and that too in the English language.

The *Balory* lived up to its reputation. Some of the crew went missing at Gibraltar. A passenger fell overboard in the Red Sea. Lifeboats were lowered, but he could not be found.

Praveen fell in love with an Egyptian girl who disembarked at Aden. He followed her ashore, and I had to run after him and get him back to the ship. As we docked at Ballard Pier, a fire broke out in one of the holds, but by then we were safely ashore. Praveen was swamped by relatives who carried him off to the suburbs of Bombay. I made my way to Victoria Terminus and boarded the Dehra Dun Express. It was a slow passenger train, which went chugging through several states in the general direction of northern India. Two days and two nights later we crawled through the eastern Doon. It was early March. The mango trees were in blossom, the peacocks were calling, and Belsize Park was far away.